THE SPIDER:
DEATH REIGN OF THE VAMPIRE KING

THE SPIDER

MASTER OF MEN!

DEATH REIGN OF THE VAMPIRE KING

By Grant Stockbridge

STEEGER BOOKS • 2020

CHAPTER 1
THE BAT MAN

TWENTY MEN with shotguns patrolled the wide lawns of Robert Latham's mansion crouching in the black shadows of night. Their hands were tightly clamped on their weapons and they cringed close against the walls of the house. They watched the moon-drenched sky fearfully.

From the dense shadow of a shrub a score of yards away, another man spied upon them. He was a hunched, grotesque figure and his long black cape made his body blend with the darkness. He held no weapon, but beside him was a large bird cage. On his lips was a thin, tight smile....

Those guards feared different terror, but if they could have seen this lurking man, they would have fled screaming in panic behind the protecting walls of the house. Not even their ready shotguns would have reassured them. For they were men of the Underworld and he who watched preyed upon their kind. He slew and left a mocking vermilion seal upon their foreheads to show that full vengeance had been exacted by the champion of oppressed humanity—nemesis of all criminals—the Spider!

The smile lingered on the Spider's lips as he surveyed the mansion, blazing with a hundred lights, and watched the men move about furtively with their deadly guns. He was determined to enter that house, though he knew that discovery within those walls would mean certain death at the hands of these men whose

Men and women rushed from the theatre into the attack of myriads of vampire bats!

fear of him was matched only by their hatred and their desire to kill him. Yes, his entrance must be secret... for a while.

The Spider rose slowly to his full, bowed height, lifted the cage at arm's length and removed its bottom. For perhaps thirty seconds, nothing happened at all; then a black form dropped from the cage, spread leathery wings and flitted off erratically into the night. Then another and another, until six bats had taken wing. The Spider laid the cage gently on the earth, crouched again into the shadows to wait. The lights of the mansion would attract insects and those bats fed on small, flying vermin of the night. When the bats flitted between those men and the sky, the panic of terror would reign....

The Spider nodded. They had reason for fright, these men. Within two weeks, a dozen race-horses and four men who frequented the tracks had been killed by the bite of vampire bats!

Useless to say that vampire bats never had been known outside of the tropics; useless to state that they never killed. There could be no mistaking the type of wound, the tiny area of skin peeled away by the keen, painless teeth of tile bat. But the bodies of the victims had not been drained of blood. They died instead... *of poison!*

The Spider smiled coldly in the darkness. His bats were not poisonous—not even vampires—but the men who watched the home of Robert Latham would not know that....

Abruptly, one of the armed guards cried out shrilly. There was more than warning in the shout. There was panic, fear and dread. His shotgun belched flame and lead upward into the darkness; then another man also screamed and fired. A ground floor door flung open in the mansion and the men streaked toward it, shotguns bellowing.

THIS WAS the moment for which the Spider had played. He wrapped his cape tightly about his body lest its flapping betray him and ran fleetly forward. When he burst into the moonlit ring about the house, he was shouting more loudly than any of the other panic-stricken men. He went in through the door with the rest, mistaken momentarily for one of their number.

Swiftly, he backed across the room in which the terrified guards were huddling. A man turned toward him:

"Geez!" he gulped, "the boss was right. Them bats—"

So much he said before he realized that this sinister, capped man with the hunched shoulders—with cold eyes gleaming beneath the wide brim of a black slouch hat—was no comrade of his. His mouth opened to cry out. His eyes stretched and terror glanced across his countenance. The Spider was recognized!

If this man shouted aloud the Spider's name, a dozen shotguns would blaze at once. These men feared him, but like cornered rats, they would shoot him down....

The Spider's action was as swift as his thought. His left hand shot forward, the first two fingers rigidly pointed. They struck basic nerve centers in the throat. With the cry unuttered on his lips, the man collapsed. In two leaping strides, the Spider crossed the room, plunged through a door. The other men, staring fearfully out into the darkness, while the last of the guards still raced for cover from the threat of those harmless bats the Spider had loosed, saw nothing, knew nothing of the mere frightful menace among them until they turned and saw their companion on the floor. Even then they did not understand, but cried that bats—the vampire bats—had slain again!

Within the house, crouching now in the shadow of a stairway, the Spider heard that cry with tightened lips that knew no mirth. If the gods were good, he would find here tonight an answer to this mystery of vampire bats whose bite was fatal. Newspapers, even reputable scientists, talked of a new species of bat carrying the poisoned fangs of snakes….

The Spider, waiting there in the darkness for the excitement to die, shook his head slowly. There had been other such foolish theories as this whenever the criminal great turned their hands to slaughter. In his many battles to protect mankind against them, the Spider had unearthed drugs that drove men mad, and others that made them docile as dogs; explosives which performed the impossible by absolutely disintegrating whatever they blasted; there had been a gas that destroyed steel as termites do wooden beams… And now there were vampire bats which killed like snakes! No, he did not believe in such vermin. There was something far more menacing behind this nascent terror than a new species of bat.

The Spider was ever alert for new outbreaks of crime. It was only by constant vigilance that he had averted, a dozen times over, the desire of the underworld to rule over the nation; the slaughter of untold thousands… It had seemed to him now that perhaps some ring of race-track gamblers had conceived a

6

new, horrible weapon and was using it, at present, to destroy personal enemies and to frame races. If that were true, it was no more than a routine job for the police; but suppose… suppose the criminals behind this strange new terror, turned their thoughts to nation-wide conquest!

The Spider had seen many overwhelming reigns of terror begin thus trivially. He had learned the wisdom of striking quickly and terribly. So he had come tonight to determine what Latham knew of this strange, new, killing instrument.

The turmoil below was quieting. Soon the patrol of the grounds would begin again. The Spider had no fear that the man he had struck would regain consciousness and betray him. The *jiu-jitsu* blow would be effective for at least an hour and by that time, the Spider's presence would be known to them all!

A SLOW smile crossed the Spider's straight lips as he crept stealthily up the service stairway of the mansion toward the second floor sitting room, where, he knew, Latham kept his watch. There was a shotgun guard in the wide, upper hall. The Spider drew a length of silken line from a pocket of his cape, rope less than the diameter of a pencil which yet had a tensile strength of seven hundred pounds! The Spider's web, police had dubbed it. Well, he would use it now to catch a fly!

Carefully, he looped the cord, carefully tossed it. The unwary guard felt gossamer brush his throat; then he was yanked off his feet, his shotgun clattering to the floor. The Spider was beside him in an instant and once more he struck swiftly to render the man unconscious. He freed his line and, in two long bounds, was at the door behind which Latham lurked with his bodyguard.

That noise of clattering gun had been intentional. After its sound, all was utter, waiting silence. Then, abruptly, the door the Spider watched snapped open. A man with a gun held rigidly ready sprang out into the hall. He grated a curse as he saw the prostrate guard, moved toward him cautiously. The Spider's fist lashed out, caught him hard on the jaw. While the man still wavered on his feet, the Spider had yanked away his gun, was through the open door, had closed it, and the automatic was covering the room.

"Ah, Latham," said the Spider, his voice flat, mocking. "Let me compliment you on the efficacy of your guard!" He laughed softly, and that sound, too, was taunting, blood-chilling.

There were three men in the room and they sat—one of them half-stood—in attitudes of frozen fright. Only Latham's gun was in sight, upon a small, nearby taboret which also held whiskey and a soda siphon. He held a glass in his right hand and, the first to recover; he began presently to slosh the liquid about in it slowly. He was spare, but full-faced, and distinguished with his smooth, brown hair which had whitened upon the temples.

"Damn' glad you've come, Spider," Latham said calmly. "Perhaps you know some way of stopping these damned bats."

"Just keep on drinking, Latham," the Spider said. "I wouldn't think of interrupting your pleasure."

The Spider's voice was gentle, but the grim, gaunt face with its lipless mouth and harsh beak of a nose was threat enough.

Latham gazed at the sallow face, the hunch-backed figure in black cape that crouched behind the ready gun and his pale face became grayish. His glass moved jerkily away from the taboret and he touched tongue to his dry lips.

"Good God, Spider," he said hoarsely, "I… I was just going to set my glass down."

"Certainly, Latham," the Spider agreed.

"Tonight, Latham, you have no reason to fear me. I simply want to ask you some questions… *Whose stable shelters the vampire bats?*"

Latham contrived a smile. "The guard I've got here tonight should prove to you that mine doesn't, Spider," he said anxiously. "Hell, my men just drove away one attack…!"

The Spider's lipless mouth parted a little, but he did not explain the bats. Abruptly, tension whipped his body. He half-crouched and his gun jutted toward Latham's chest. Pounding footsteps were racing down the hall. In the darkness outside, a man screamed—a cry that choked off in mid-shout. With the suddenness of lightning, the lights clicked out and somewhere, wailing, quavering through the night, came a mourning note that was like the moan of a tortured soul in hell.

"Oh God!" screamed Latham. "It's the Bat Man!"

FOR FIFTEEN seconds after the first beat of footsteps, the Spider had suspected a trick. Perhaps someone knew the method of quickly reviving the man he had knocked out. There was a way… But the sound of Latham's voice, the inarticulate fright in the cries of the others, convinced him that their terror was genuine.

9

Richard Wentworth

The Bat Man… no need to inquire what they meant. He had suspected human agency behind the attacks of the vampire bats. These men knew and they called the master of the winged killers… *the Bat Man!*

The Spider waited tensely for this oddly-named man to show himself. His guns were ready… Instantly, instinctively, the Spider had sprung from the spot he stood when the lights went out, but no one moved to attack him. There was a wild stampede of feet toward the door. Latham cried out.

"Keep that door shut, damn you!" His gun streaked flame out of the darkness. Near the door, a man groaned and thumped to the floor.

"Keep away from that door!" Latham shouted again, his panic barely under control. "I'll shoot the first man who touches it."

The Spider realized abruptly that the running in the hall had ceased. Either the man had seen the bodies there and fled in terror, or… *or the bats already had struck!* The Spider crouched to the floor, so that he caught the gray light of the window across the room—so that he could watch movement about him. No one budged. A man whimpered off to his right near the door and the one who had fallen at Latham's shot breathed with rattling breath. Latham had aimed well. He was cursing monotonously.

"You see, Spider," he whispered. "You see, he's after me. The Bat Man…!"

His voice was drowned in the bellowing blasts of shotguns just outside the window. There was a tearing, ripping sound of

wire screen and the Spider saw against the gray square of the window the fluttering form of a bat!

"Cover your throat, Latham!" he shouted. "A bat just came in the window."

Even as he cried the warning, a half dozen more of the black, loathsome things dodged in through the torn screening. A shuddering moan came from Latham.

"You can't tell when they bite," he whimpered. "You can't tell. Oh, God…!"

With his teeth set, the Spider whipped out his fountain pen flashlight, squeezed out its widely diffused ray. He saw a dodging leathery-winged beast within inches of his face. The bat flicked away, but the Spider's bullet was swifter than its flight. The creature was torn to bits by forty-five caliber lead and the Spider pressed back against the wall, watching, watching….

Abruptly, he became aware of two things. Within the house, all was silence. And there, but dimly heard, came a shrill, monstrous squeaking, as if a giant bat called to its kind!

It sounded again and black bat forms fluttered through the beam of the Spider's light, whirled toward the window and were gone.

One more of the creatures the Spider smashed with lead; then he was alone with the thumping of his heart, the reverberations of his shot. He lifted his gloved left hand and touched away the moisture that had oozed out through his facial make-up. He acknowledged to himself that in those few seconds, crouched against the wall, he had known the cold touch of fear. Bats with poisoned teeth…! He fought down a shudder.

On swift, silent feet, the Spider crossed the room and peered out of the window. The entire mansion was dark and on the grounds nothing visible moved. The squeaking which clearly had recalled the bats had now ceased and far off, toward where the moon sank, a dog howled. Upward, there was nothing except the blackness of the sky… Suddenly, the Spider's teeth shut upon a curse, his guns swirled upward. But he knew that shooting would be vain. His eyes were narrow as he stared….

NO BAT ever had that wing spread, nor flew with that gliding, motionless ease. And yet, sliding effortlessly across the starry sky, the Spider beheld a creature *with bat wings fully ten feet across!*

Even as he watched, the thing steeped its angle of dive and sped out of sight over the close, clustering trees that reached upward toward the sky. For long moments after it was gone, the Spider crouched there at the window. He was aware of his quickened breath, of the aching in the forearm of the hand that held his gun.

"It was out of range," he whispered to himself. "Out of range!"

He jerked his head angrily, reached up a gloved hand to shut the window, then turned back to the room. Almost the Spider doubted his eyesight. No, no, he had *seen* the thing. His eyes had been too well trained in a thousand situations where life and liberty, a thousand lives, hinged on the accuracy of his vision. Breath hissed noisily out between his teeth. Latham had cried, "The Bat Man!" Was it possible that what he had seen was a… a man with wings!

The Spider spread the light of his torch over the floor. There was no doubt in his own mind of what he would find, but the horror written largely on Latham's twisted features tightened his own grim mouth. Latham had covered his throat, so the bat had fastened to his hand. He was dead.

Slowly, the Spider turned the beam upon the other two in the room. They were dead, too. He found the instrument which had smashed out the screening of the window—a spear with a special collar of light, steel blades which extended fully nine inches all around the haft. It must have been hurled with terrific force, for the screening was double, a heavier screen mesh outside the usual lighter wire.

The Spider made his way swiftly through the darkened house, avoiding the bodies of men that were everywhere scattered in distorted, tortured attitudes of death. There was no use in carrying the bats he had killed with him. He had recognized them as vampires of an ordinary variety, *Desmodus rufus*, a tiny creature whose body was no more than three inches long, with a wing spread of only seven inches. He could recognize it by its reddish-brown body and the black wings with edging of white. The heavy bullet had smashed the animal too badly for him to examine its teeth. However, that was scarcely necessary. The Spider was terribly sure now that human agency was behind the murders.

At the outer door, the Spider paused for a moment, his eyes dark and narrow. Twenty-seven men had died here tonight by the bite of non-poisonous vampire bats. He himself had seen the attack. A cold fury swept him as he realized what havoc these same tactics would wreak if they were used against the populace at large. So far, the Bat Man had confined his attacks to a few gamblers, also creatures of the half-world like the bats. The

Spider could not mourn their loss to humanity—but suppose the man went power-mad? Suppose the agency behind these attacks turned loose his murderous creatures upon cities, upon entire country sides…?

The Spider's lean, taut-skinned face set in determined lines. It was his job to keep such things from coming to pass!

His gun was in his hand as he stepped outside the door. A blazing light slapped the Spider in the face. From the close-pressing shrubbery, a man called hoarsely:

"Hands up, it's the Law!" The voice broke off in a gasp. "Good God, it's—the Spider! The Spider sent them bats!"

"That's the man," broke in a girl's voice, a deep, emotional voice.

Then another man, shrill, almost hysterical with his discovery. "It's the Spider! The Spider!"

CHAPTER 2
"DEATH TO THE SPIDER!"

THE SPIDER'S gun was ready at his side when the police behind the light challenged, but he did not fire. The Spider did not fight the law. He might go outside it in a thousand ways, kill, burglarize, kidnap… But when he did, it was to smash criminals, to assist the law in its great work, because the police and other enforcement officers were hedged in by too many restrictions to operate effectively. He would die before be would fire upon one of the law's men.

Yet capture meant death for the Spider; it meant a revelation of his real identity and disgrace for his comrades and the one woman in the world who knew his secrets, Nita van Sloan. It meant even more than that. It meant that the law, for all its myriad successes against petty, customary criminals, would be without a means of combating this new terror that had arisen from the Underworld: the Bat Man, whose existence as yet they did not even suspect!

The thoughts flashed through the Spider's brain in the second he closed the door and felt the assault of the light. Useless to attempt a retreat. Before he could open the door and duck from sight, a dozen bullets would smash through his body. There were at least twenty men in the shrubbery out there. He could hear their rustling, their murmur as his identity was shouted hoarsely into the night. He might shoot out the light. It would give him an instant. But the night was scarcely dark enough to hope that he could flee unseen.

The Spider shrugged his shoulders, dropped the gun and raised his hands shoulder-high.

"I'm the Spider, all right," he admitted calmly, "but you'll have to hunt someone else to take the blame for the bats. I thought Latham was the man, but I was wrong."

Two men were coming out from behind the light now, walking wide lest they come between the guns and the Spider.

"What do you mean, wrong?" asked the hoarse voice that first had spoken.

The Spider allowed his straight lipless mouth to twist into a smile. "You'll find out when you take a look inside."

The two men were close now. Each had fastened a handcuff

to one of his own wrists and held the other cuff open, ready for the Spider's hand. His eyes turned cold as he saw that. He could escape from handcuffs that were fastened between his own wrists, but if he were chained to two men...!

"We'll look into that," the leader growled. "But it'll take more than your say-so to clear you. This young lady seen you comin' in here with a cage... Stand still. There's ten guns on you!"

The Spider had started uncontrollably at the information that he had been seen entering the grounds. Why, this was utterly damning! How could he convince these men that the bats he had let escape had been harmless?

"Who accuses me?" he demanded sharply. "Let me see the one who accuses me?"

The leader's voice dropped a note. Never mind that now. You keep out of sight, young lady. He's up to some trick."

The Spider frowned, his heart thudding in his breast. He had had no definite plan in mind, but it was apparent these men were alert for any trick. They would be eager to kill... The two men approaching him, both of them broad, tall farmers, were within a foot or two with their ready handcuffs. They were his only chance, the Spider knew. He must somehow use these two to escape, for once those handcuffs closed about his wrists…The men behind the light were watching keenly, for they understood the situation as well as he.

THE SPIDER extended his left arm toward the man who approached from that direction, smiled at him, with a thin parting of his lips.

"Come on, come on," he said impatiently. "What are you waiting for? You couldn't be afraid of the Spider?"

The man's young face flushed a little. He braced himself visibly and, holding the handcuff in both hands, stepped within reach of the outstretched hand, slapped the shackle about the wrist and fumbled to close the cuff. It was the very instant for which the Spider had waited. By offering his wrist so placidly for the bracelet, he had partially disarmed the man. But, even more important, he had obtained a hold on one of the men before the other had quite reached a place where he could act.

While the man still fumbled with the cuff, the Spider's fingers closed upon the chain between the shackles and, without a visible preliminary tensing of muscles—without a change in his face—he yanked savagely upon the bracelets. In his timidity, the man was leaning forward off-balance and the jerk pulled him directly in front of the Spider, between him and the guns that threatened.

The second man leaped forward and the Spider slammed his captive against him, slipped his wrist from the still-unfastened cuff and skipped backward through the door into the house. An excited man fired a shotgun and one of the struggling pair cried out in pain, The Spider heard all that as he slammed and bolted the door, then he raced to a window on the same side of the building.

The law men were already battering on the door. A window had been smashed in and gunshots were pouring death into the building. Guards were racing to surround the mansion. The Spider opened his window and waited. A guard started past the casement, paused and stared at it uncertainly, then inched forward. The silken rope snaked out of the darkness, yanked him to the window. A single blow knocked him out and the Spider was through the window and away....

Once he was amid the shrubbery and trees, he was safe. Not even his namesake, the spider, could move more soundlessly than he. At the high, iron fence that surrounded the estate, he whistled softly in a weird, minor key. Seconds later, a shadow glided to the opposite side of the fence and a rope ladder, made of the same soft, silken cord, came swinging over. A moment later, he was speeding with that other shadow beside him, toward the hidden lane where he had parked the car.

"Wah! *Sahib!*" whispered the one beside him, "are we mice that we flee from battle!" He spoke in the Hindustani that was native to him.

The Spider chuckled. "They are men of the law. Ram Singh, more to be pitied for their stupidity than slain."

The turbaned Hindu, the Spider's servant to the death, grunted, but made no other reply. To Ram Singh, all men who opposed his master were game for his swift, keen knives. *Wah!* Mice!

The Spider flung into a black, low-swung Daimler sedan

and the Hindu leaped to the driver's seat, sent the powerful car almost silently through the woods lane. In the tonneau, the Spider dropped his hand to a button beneath the left half of the cushions. The seat slid smoothly forward, turned half about and revealed in its back a closely hung wardrobe. The Spider folded upward a mirror about which neon lights instantly glowed. He pulled out a tray fined with the equipment of disguise....

FIVE MINUTES later, as the car slid to the concrete highway which skirted the front of Latham's estate, the Spider—who was the Spider no longer—slid the cleverly contrived wardrobe into place, lounged back against the luxurious upholstery and drew a cigarette from a platinum case. When the police stopped him a hundred yards further on, he leaned forward politely to speak to the sergeant.

"Identify myself?" he said in the rich baritone that was his natural voice. "Oh, decidedly, sergeant!" He drew out a wallet, extracted a card and presented it between two perfectly manicured fingers.

The sergeant scowled at first, then his face cleared. He actually smiled. "A thousand pardons, Mr. Wentworth," he murmured obsequiously. "I've heard of you up in New York, working with the cops to stop some of them crooks. Something here might interest you, sir. Them vampire bats killed about twenty men over there...."

Richard Wentworth listened attentively. This was no masquerade, but his true identity. Scion of a wealthy—it's last surviving member—he had long ago pledged himself to the suppression of crime, he had created that other sinister char-

acter, the Spider, so
that the Underworld
might be additionally
cleansed by a healthy
fear.

Richard Went-
worth, clubman,
sportsman and
amateur criminolo-
gist, was a friend of
Governors and of Presidents, a man eagerly sought after by
Commissioners of Police whenever the ugly head of super-
crime was lifted. He sat there, his bronzed, strongly chiseled
face keenly intelligent as he listened to the sergeant's account
of the deaths at Latham's Mansion. Finally he nodded gravely,
a pleasant smile on his firm lips, his gray-blue eyes merry.

"Thank you, sergeant," he said, "if you will pass me through
the gates I would be glad to look over the scene."

It was wasted time, Wentworth—the Spider—knew, but it
would be suspicious to pass without inquiry. He hurried the
inspection as much as possible, on fire with eagerness to pursue
his quest. It was pretty well known in police circles that Latham
had a tie-up with Red Cullihane, a Philadelphia brewer who in
prohibition days had been one of the leading big-shots of the
East. Wentworth no longer believed that Latham was connected
with the Bat Man, but it was pretty obvious that Latham had
been a target for especial animosity. It might well be that Cullihane would next be the target.

After leaving the grounds, he stopped once on the way northward through Maryland to send a night-letter. It began *Ma Cherie* and was addressed to Miss Nita van Sloan, Riverside Towers, New York City. Part of the message said *Dinner Thursday at the Early Quaker.* The rest of it seemed to be lovers' words but actually it bade the woman he loved—his ablest ally in the battle against crime—to hasten to Philadelphia with his speedy Northrup plane and bring with her his chauffeur, Jackson, who was much more than a chauffeur in the plans of the Spider.

Then the low, black car of the Spider sped northward again. To anyone who gazed upon the man in its back seat, he would have seemed a bored member of the class of idle rich. To be sure there was a strength and intelligence about his face and a singular directness of gaze, a confidence of bearing that had nothing to do with a bank account, which might have surprised the onlooker. But, certainly, his face gave no evidence of the grim thoughts that were racing through his mind....

UNTIL NOW, Wentworth had had little opportunity to consider the events of the evening and now that he reviewed the attack of the bats, he felt a mounting sense of dread. There could be no doubt at all of human agency. Even without the wailing cry which had heralded the attack, the shrill squeaking as of a giant bat which had called the killers home, there was the spear which had smashed through the screening so that the bats would be able to enter and do their assassin's work. Yes, in that one venture, the Spider had confirmed his fear that a new menace had arisen for humanity.

Wentworth glanced at his watch, then leaned forward to

turn on the radio. There was a news broadcast about now… The announcer's voice came to him with unexpected harshness. There was excitement beneath the calm ordering of carefully enunciated syllables:

"Jack Harkins, ladies and gentlemen, bringing you the extraordinary news of the day…."

Innocuous phrases, but the man's words were fraught with tension, with terror. Harkins had a stimulating voice. He talked in pounding short phrases that seemed to bring the action he described into the very room with his listeners.

"Does the world face another of those overwhelming madman's attacks which have struck terror to our hearts in recent years? May God in His mercy will that it is not so. But it looks as if it is. These winged horrors of the night, the vampire bats, have struck again'! Twice tonight, in two widely separated parts of the country, they have struck. And, ladies and gentlemen, *one hundred and ninety-five people are dead!* Think of it, one hundred and ninety-five!"

Wentworth, listening to the hurried, staccato rhythm of the newsman, felt his hands clench in hard white knots. None could have detected the idler in his face now, for it was white and rigid with anger and his blue-gray eyes were almost black with fury. Then what he feared had already come to pass! The Bat Man had not been content with his attack upon Latham….

"At first there seemed to be no danger except to those who were associated with horses in some way. It is a well-known fact that the vampire bat confines itself largely to horses, prefers their blood to most others. But tonight, that hopeful idea was

The Spider's gun flicked out
and the policemen collapsed!

dispelled once and for all, and terribly dispelled. In Centertown, Pennsylvania, the bats flittered down and kissed the throats of lovers in the parks, they tasted of the blood of brave policemen on their beats, brought their poison death to the gay crowd before the motion picture shows. A dozen people were killed in the panic, in the dash to escape, but many, many more were prey to the vicious poisoned teeth of these bloodthirsty little beasts...."

There was more, much more of that sort of thing, all melodramatic, highly colored and calculated to help the work of the Bat Man, whatever that was, by spreading the terror of the bats. Wentworth shook his head. There was no reason for the Spider to visit Centertown. Nothing to be gained by gazing on more bat-slain human beings. He must hasten to Philadelphia, hoping against hope that he had guessed right about the next target of the Bat Man. Abruptly his attention was pulled back to the radio....

"And now, folks, to the most exciting part of the whole thing," the newsman went on. "And something you won't know whether to believe or not. The Spider was seen at Latham's place. Yes, sir, the Spider! And a girl whose brother was killed a week ago by the bats, says she saw the Spider *carrying a cage full of bats!* Now, what does that mean? Is it possible that the Spider...."

With a grated curse, Wentworth shut off the radio and sat rigidly, staring straight ahead of him into the blackness of the night. No need to ask what lay ahead. Once more the nation would go mad and hunt the only man who could save it from the monster who had loosed his flying killers on the people. It would blame the Spider and throughout the country would ring the blood-thirsty cry of....

"Death to the Spider!"

A HARD bitterness descended upon Wentworth. Damnable to have the very people for whom he had sacrificed so much—for whom he hourly risked death and disgrace—turn upon him in this way. He should have become accustomed to it by now, he who had served without stint in the face of persecution by law and criminal and civilian, but somehow the thought could still rankle. Not that the Spider ever wavered in his devotion to the pledge he had made so long ago....

He caught up the speaking tube which communicated with Ram Singh. "I must be in Philadelphia within the hour," he ordered quietly.

He saw the tensing of the Hindu's broad shoulders, saw the turbaned head bend a little more over the steering wheel and heard the bass thunder of the engine deepen a full tone. The wind whispered past the car, but there was no other indication of its great speed except the occasional whine of tires on a curb. Within the hour. Yes, it was necessary to hurry. Wentworth had not anticipated that the Bat Man would strike again so quickly. Now that he had shown his versatility, there was no reason why he should not attack Red Cullihane, Latham's associate, at once.

Wentworth realized that it was merely his assumption that Cullihane would be attacked, a slim thread of hope. But there was no other clue to follow. It was desperately necessary that he find some more definite lead to this Bat Man immediately.

If he could only be on the scene when next the vampires struck, he had a plan....

When Ram Singh drew the powerful Daimler to a halt on a street that paralleled Philadelphia's waterfront, it was not Wentworth who alighted from the car, but a hunched and sinister figure whose very appearance was a threat... the Spider. The Spider knew—it was a part of his self-imposed duty to know—much about Red Cullihane. He knew of his home in the Heights and his gambling salon near the Early Quaker hotel where Wentworth had appointed a meeting with Nita the next evening. Actually it had been Latham who ran the place with Cullihane to provide protection.

Then there was a great, gaunt warehouse upon the hill overlooking the Quaker which was used as a depot for distribution of the Golden Stein beer which Cullihane now manufactured legally. It was this warehouse which Wentworth now approached for here was Cullihane's stronghold and, if he feared attack, it was the place where he would be most likely to barricade himself.

Swiftly, the Spider advanced on the building, invisible in the black shadows with which he merged himself, and, from an alley mouth across the street from Cullihane's warehouse, he stood watching. Three minutes passed and a black coupé cruised slowly past, turned a corner beside the warehouse and vanished. Four minutes later, it appeared again and followed the same course. The Spider's thinned lips parted a little, showing the white gleam of his teeth. He was right then. Cullihane was frightened. He had taken up his position here and the coupé was a patrol, a sentry on wheels, against attack.

When the coupé had crawled out of sight again, Wentworth darted across the street....

"Spider!" It was a woman's voice, high, challenging.

Wentworth did not turn toward the call. It was too old a trick, that crying a name to attract attention, to cause a moment of motionless waiting while deadly lead was poured into a victim. He went flat down on the pavement of the street. The crack of a light automatic sounded strangely loud in the deserted street. The bullet splatted against the bricks of the warehouse. He had a moment to wonder at the attack, then he sprang to his feet. Jumping sideways, as the girl fired again, he charged straight toward her!

DANGEROUS WORK this, racing into the muzzle of an automatic, even though it was light in caliber and a woman handled it. But like everything the Spider did, it was a maneuver shrewdly planned in his lightning-swift mind. There was no cover for him there in the middle of the street. Within seconds, Cullihane's sentry would arrive at the scene. Only one chance and he took it, charging straight on the gun.

He had two hopes, one that his charge would confuse the girl. The other... With his left arm, he billowed his cape wide to that side. In the darkness his long cape, which almost swept the ground, would make him a confusing target as it spread out to one side—would make it hard for anyone to judge the position of his body.

The muffling folds of the cape served him in good stead. His

29

charge did not frighten the girl, nor did the booming discharges of his automatic which he fired deliberately wide. But the cloak did the trick. The Spider felt two bullets tug at it. The failure of those bullets did what his charge could not. It terrified the girl. While the Spider was still twenty feet away, she turned and fled….

Wentworth raced after her, his feet silent while hers beat a panicky tattoo upon the cement. The Spider's jaw was tight set. He sprinted at his best pace and in his university days, Wentworth had broken an intercollegiate record! There was desperate need for haste. Any moment now, that prowling coupé with its two men, undoubtedly heavily armed, would be upon them. And that must not happen. It must not….

The girl twisted her head about as she ran, saw his figure with the cape streaming from broad shoulders as he rapidly overtook her. She screamed, high, piercing sounds of terror. She fired blindly, uselessly behind her… and the Spider pounced upon her. He knocked the gun arm up, slapped an arm about her waist. He did not check his speed, but lifted her bodily from the ground and sprang toward a doorway a half dozen feet ahead.

Even while he hastened for the shadows that would mean life or death to them, the girl began to struggle. She could not strike with her fists, since her back was toward Wentworth, but she did use her feet. Her heels drummed against his shins. The Spider could hear the roar of the engine as the automobile he feared raced to the scene. He heard the squeal of skidding tires… With a vaulting leap, he gained the doorway, thrust the girl into a corner and held her there.

"If you move, you die," he ordered sharply—and realized his mistake. The two men—the coupé which had rushed up the street—was not the patrol at the warehouse. It was a police radio-car with two uniformed men in it. But the Spider's action, his order, caught them unaware. They had both jumped from the car, both stood beside it. And though they held guns in hand, the Spider's weapons alone were ready to shoot. They could not know that he would not fire on them.

"This way," Wentworth ordered tightly. "Drop those guns and walk this way."

Their recognition was apparent in the whiteness of their faces. They hesitated, their guns tightly clenched. Wentworth saw the struggle in their faces. Should they submit, or lift guns and shoot it out with this arch-killer? If they were lucky enough to win in the gun battle, untold rewards would be theirs. Fifty thousand dollars had been posted on the Spider's head. There would be promotion....

Wentworth's left hand automatic spat flame and the gun flew from one policeman's hand, rattled against the coupé. He gripped his numbed arm, cursing.

"Drop that gun!" Wentworth ordered again, quietly.

The second policeman obeyed and the two moved slowly toward the Spider at his order. Wentworth's eyes were probing the darkness beyond them. Where were Cullihane's two killers in the other coupé? Obvious that they had ducked out of the way when the police car had shown up, running silent under orders. But the men would not have gone far. They were even more vitally interested in the cause of the shooting than the police....

Wentworth's hope lay in the throbbing police-car at the curb. If he could get the girl into that, escape would be certain. The girl, whose identity he did not yet know, might yield some secret.... The Spider became abruptly aware that the eyes of one of the police had flashed to the doorway behind him and that now the man was doing his best to pretend he had not looked there at all.

There was but one explanation. The girl was creeping out of the doorway, still bent on his destruction, as she had been when first her gun had spat at his back. Yet he could not turn to meet her with these two police before him. He could hear the girl's shoes making small rasping noises on the gritty pavement. Damn it, why couldn't she use sense? If she jumped him from behind....

He shook his head. If she jumped him from behind, she would succeed in what she wished. She would achieve the Spider's death. She herself would suffer nothing. The footsteps crept closer....

CHAPTER 3
THE WINGED DEATH AGAIN

THE TWO policemen now needed no prompting to move toward the Spider. Both had seen the girl creeping upon him from behind and they wanted to be near enough to attack when she distracted the Spider's attention. He let them come while he listened acutely to the girl's stealthy approach. There was a way out, but it would have to be perfectly timed....

The footsteps of the girl were very close now. One more step and she would probably leap upon him. The final step was delayed and, with a quick tensing of muscles, the Spider lunged to the side while his guns swung with alert readiness on the two police. He was just in time. Even as he sprang, the girl catapulted herself upon the spot where he had stood. Thrown off balance, she reeled against one of the police and the two sprawled together to the pavement.

Wentworth turned the flurry to his own account. With a quick stride, he was beside them. His gun flicked out and the policeman collapsed, unconscious, upon the pavement. The second man sprang to the attack, but stopped a blow which felled him also.

The Spider took handcuffs and uniform caps from the policemen, jerked the girl to her feet and thrust her into the coupé. He secured her to the door post with the handcuffs, then sprang behind the wheel, hurled the car forward and traveled at maximum speed for a half dozen blocks before he cut the pace. He put one of the uniform caps upon the girl's fluffy, black hair, pulled the other down over his own head. The interior was dark and it was unlikely that anyone would see more than the silhouette of the occupants' heads. It would prevent detection for a short while. He glanced toward the girl. She sat rigidly, staring straight ahead. Her jaw was set and there was furious anger in her face. She was surprisingly pretty in that moment... abruptly the Spider recognized her. She was the girl who had accused him at Latham's place, whose brother, according to the radio had been killed by bats. But how in the world had she come here so swiftly? How had she known so accurately where to lay her ambush? Wentworth's pulses quickened. Did not all this mean that she was an ally… of the Bat Man? He must find out. Even her brother's death did not preclude the possibility. He turned to the girl.

"Your name, as I recall it," Wentworth said quietly, "is June Calvert. What was your brother's name, Miss Calvert?"

The girl jerked her head about toward him. "Have you killed so many that you can't remember the names of your victims?" she demanded, her deep voice vibrant.

"I didn't kill your brother," Wentworth said. "If I had, I should not bother to deny it. There are enough kills on my conscience to make one more unimportant."

The girl's lips curled though her face was very white. "You have the courage to sit there and admit… admit…!"

"Those I kill always richly deserve death," said the Spider. "I did not kill your brother."

Something in his quiet tone seemed to pierce the girl's contempt and anger. The contempt left her face, leaving in its place a puzzled question.

"I saw you with a cage of bats," she said. "Bob Latham… I thought he might have a hand in Dick's death, I was going there to… to… I saw you with the bats."

Wentworth nodded slowly. "Yes, but if you saw, you also saw that none of my bats killed. It was fully half an hour after I went into the house that the vampire bats came. Mine were ordinary insect-eating bats that I captured to create a diversion there and open a path for my entrance."

His quiet manner seemed to be convincing the girl against her will. June Calvert's head sagged forward, her chin trembled.

"If you know anything about me at all, Miss Calvert," Wentworth continued quietly, "you must know that the Spider keeps his oath. I give you my word of honor that I did not kill your brother. I give you my word, also, to kill the man who *is* responsible!"

SLOWLY, THE girl's head came up. She turned her dark, intent eyes upon him, her wrists, bound by the handcuffs to the doorpost, closed and opened nervously.

"But why," she whispered, "why are you trying so to convince me? If, as you say, you have already killed so many, how does one accusation more or less affect it?" The Spider had his eyes on the street in the flash of the headlights. He laughed shortly, bitterly.

"I do not mind just accusations," he said, "but when they are false…" He shrugged. "You will hear plenty against me from now on. You will hear that I am responsible for all the deaths that occur from these poisonous bats. Even when I kill the Bat Man himself, the idea of my guilt will not be entirely dispelled… Oh, forget it! Will you tell me how you happened to be waiting there for me?"

The girl lifted her shoulders in a slight shrug. "There is no magic in it," she said. "I knew that Cullihane and Latham were allies. Because Latham was attacked by the bats, I thought Cullihane would be also. I thought you'd be there to…."

The girl broke off as a shrill, rising whine came from the radio beneath the dashboard of the car. It ended and the announcer's dry voice intoned a call.

"Call two-thirty-five, car two three five, go to Seventy-first and Sullivan streets. Bat scare. That is...."

The announcer's voice broke off in the middle of the signature, then came in again, stronger, more alert.

"Calling all cars. Five men killed by bats at Seventy-first and Sullivan streets. Cars two-three-five, one-seven-four, Cruiser one-eight, go to Seventy-First and Sullivan...."

A ragged curse forced itself out between Wentworth's locked teeth. Even as he feared, the Bat Man had struck again at once. The plans that he had laid for tracing the killers was nullified by a simple lack of time. A new thought struck him. The new point of attack where five citizens had been killed by the poison bats was nowhere near the warehouse of Cullihane, nor any other of his strongholds. Why then had the bats been loosed?

Wentworth started to whirl the car to race toward the spot where the bats were killing. That movement undoubtedly saved his life. From behind him Game a stuttering drum roll of gunfire. Bullets tore the side of the car, pocked the windshield, then smashed it into glittering, slashing fragments. A shard stung his cheek... The Spider glimpsed his assailants in the rear-vision mirror, but already he was in action. He cramped the wheels of the car still further and drove head on for a building on his right. The car behind him was Cullihane's prowl coupé. The men in it were still shooting. They must either have spotted him, or revived the police and learned from them that it was the Spider who kept watch.

As the coupé dove head-on for the building, Wentworth shouted to the girl to crouch to the floor and himself slid down behind the wheel, stomped his foot on the brakes. The force of the collision with the building wall half-stunned him, but the attacking car was already roaring away, convinced its work was done. Wentworth slapped open the door, leveled one automatic and fired three times carefully.

The gun car went out of control, skidded into a side street, and out of sight, hit something with a loud, splintering crash. Under the dash board of Wentworth's car, the radio was still squawking....

"Calling all cars! Calling all cars!" the announcer's voice was harsh and excited. "Close all windows. Patrol cars put up curtains. Kill bats when possible. Warn all pedestrians to get behind closed doors at first opportunity. Twenty-two have been reported dead from the bats…!"

WENTWORTH'S TEETH locked. His eyes were hot flames. He freed June Calvert from the handcuffs. "Get under cover at once," he ordered.

He raced away from the wreck. He would have to cover a dozen blocks before be could reach his own car. Talking with June Calvert, he had traveled further than be had thought away from where he had left his own car. Small chance that he'd be able to get a taxicab… He became abruptly aware that June Calvert was running after him. The sound of her limping steps, one foot encased in a shoe, the other only stockinged, was close behind, Wentworth whirled.

"Get to cover," he ordered. "You must protect yourself or those bats…."

The girl stooped and snatched off her other shoe, came on toward him in her stocking feet. Her eyes were wide, determined.

"Wherever the bats are," she said, panting a little "will be the killer of my brother. I'm going with you."

There was no time to argue with her. With a shrug, Wentworth turned and hurried on, hearing the quickened breath of the girl beside him. He kept an alert lookout for a cab, but none appeared. He ran lightly, conserving wind and strength. The girl presented a problem in more ways than one. If he reached his car, with her still beside him….

He sprang out into a cross street and halted, pivoting to the left. His Daimler was there, rolling softly swift, toward him with Ram Singh behind the wheel. But he could not permit the Hindu to greet him lest the girl who had proved herself shrewd enough to anticipate the Spider's next move, suspect his true identity.

Wentworth flipped an automatic into his palm, pointed it at Ram Singh and ordered him to halt. For a moment, surprise glared from the Hindu's eyes, then the girl burst out from behind the corner and he understood. His jaw trembled in simulated fear as he drew the car to a halt for Wentworth and the girl to enter. "Don't shoot, mister," he pleaded.

Wentworth hid a smile as he motioned June Calvert into the car, climbed in himself.

"I see there's a radio here," he said dryly, "Turn it on and let's see where the fight is the thickest."

Wentworth felt a keen disappointment while his heart was wrung with pity, with a bitter fury, at the knowledge of what must be happening here in this city at the moment with the winged death of the Bat Man fluttering from the sky. He had not anticipated any such wholesale attack as this, but he had expected Cullihane's place to be assailed by the Bat Man. He had hoped that when it happened be would be in a position to put a certain plan into effect, but this surprise assault had left him without recourse. Nita and his plane were far away....

The radio came in with the clicking of the button, "…all cars. Calling all cars. Spider reported seen in neighborhood of Water Street and Sycamore. Suspected of connection with the vampire bats...."

Wentworth's laughter was sharp and bitter. He was always fugitive from the law, but now once more the entire forces of a hundred cities, of the nation, would concentrate on his capture while the real persons behind the depredations of the bats went unhampered. Once more, it would depend on the Spider alone to find and destroy this new and overweening menace to the nation—handicapped by a thousand enemies bent upon his death. How the Bat Man must be laughing now!

THE RADIO was squawking without ceasing. New reports of the bats sweeping death over the city. Now they were on Walnut Hill, now at Twelfth and Market streets… As that last message came through, Wentworth leaned forward toward Ram Singh on whose back he kept the automatic centered.

"Get to Twelfth and Market streets at once," he ordered flatly. "And make it fast or I'll give you a slug in the back to remember me by."

Ram Singh sent the Daimler hurtling through the streets. Wentworth leaned back against the cushions, apparently relaxed. He fingered a cigarette from a platinum case and lighted it with a snap of a lighter. Outwardly calm, he was aflame with anger. Twelfth and Market! It was in the heart of the downtown section. A few blocks away, the theaters would be loosing their gay crowds into the streets. There would be a mighty harvest for the bats this night, unless, unless....

He leaned forward. "That cigar store on the corner. Stop there!" he commanded sharply.

He handed an automatic to June Calvert. "Hold the car here," he said and sprang out without waiting for parley. He knew he risked death in the moments while he raced toward the store with his back toward the girl's gun. She was still not wholly convinced of his innocence. He had read that in her eyes, but she thought it wise to go with him in hope of learning more. This opportunity with a gun in her hand.... But the Spider had not acted without forethought. The very fact of his arming her and turning his back would militate against her suspicions. Wouldn't she hesitate to shoot a man who trusted her?

The drug clerk pulled up a startled head as a hunched figure in a black cape went past him toward the phone booths. He kept staring as Wentworth dropped a coin and dialed a number. The

Spider watched him through the door which he opened just enough to extinguish the light within the booth. If he had been recognized the police cars would soon have another errand than warning the people of the bats....

Richard Wentworth, clubman and dilettante of the arts, was a personal friend of Commissioner Harrington of the Philadelphia police. The Spider called his home, got through to Harrington. He wasted no preliminaries.

"The Spider speaking," he announced, his voice flat, crisp. "You probably already know that the vampire bats are loose in the city. I think they are intended to attack the theater crowds. It would be wise to order all theaters to lock in their audiences until the bats are gone. You may save thousands of lives by that order...."

So much Wentworth got out in a quick rush before Harrington interrupted. The Spider smashed through his words with sharp tones of command.

"Keep quiet, fool! Seconds are precious!" he snapped. "Send out loudspeaker cars to shout warning along the streets. Get a plane with a loudspeaker if you can. Don't forget that most of your people have not had a chance yet to learn about the bats."

Harrington was sputtering with his anger now. Wentworth's lips thinned to a smile. He could imagine the expression on

Harrington's heavy face. It had been many a day, Wentworth thought, since anyone had dared to take that tone with the man. But it had served its purpose, had kept him silent while the message of the Spider was poured into his ears.

"For God's sake, act quickly," Wentworth urged, then he hung up softly and sped back out to the car. The cigar clerk stared at him, then staggered back a step against the wall. His eyes stretched wide and he pointed a trembling finger.

"The Spider," he gabbled. "The Spider!"

HE TURNED and ran toward a narrow door that opened in the back wall of the room, his voice going incoherent, turning into a hysterical scream. Before he had reached the doorway, the Spider was beside the car. He sprang into the rear, past June Calvert.

"Twelfth and Market!" he ordered again. "Split the road wide open."

He took the automatic from June's hand. Her dark eyes were frowning on him.

"What did you do?" she almost whispered.

Wentworth told her with clipped sentences while his eyes searched the way ahead.

He would do more when he reached the scene of activity, but what he wanted more than anything else was a chance to strike at the man behind these atrocities.

What was the reason behind this new threat against humanity? There could be no question that greed for money lay somewhere in the background. Money was responsible for all organized crime and, heaven knew, there was organization here—incredibly acute organization....

The Daimler was gliding through the business section of the city now, all dark save where the sparkling of theater lights threw a multi-colored glare against the heavens. A police radio-roadster, curtains tightly drawn, raced by with siren screaming and, at a word, Ram Singh followed. The radio still howled its incredibly mounting toll of deaths. Nearly a hundred human beings had been slain and the police undoubtedly could not discover more than half the victims so soon after the tragedy had begun. It was seemingly impossible that so purposeless a slaughter....

The Daimler swung a comer and a woman's screams rang out. Wentworth could see her, a dark, dodging form, as she ran frantically toward him along the street. She held a child in her arms and was bent far over it, protecting it with arms and head and bowed body. Wentworth could not see the cause of her terror, but he had no need. About her head, one of those poisonous vampires of the Bat Man must be flitting, seeking an inch of bare flesh in which to sink its deadly teeth.

Incredible that vampires should behave in this way—bats that were rarely seen, but came silently in the darkness of the night to flutter down on sleeping men and animals and take their ton of blood. But these bats were attacking as if they were hydrophobic—or as if they were starved! Yes, that must be it. Vampire bats starved until they would attack any living thing, against any odds, to obtain food!

The thought was a flash of light in Wentworth's brain. He had needed to shout no order to Ram Singh. The Daimler already was sprinting toward where the woman stumbled in a heavy, hopeless run, her screams despairing as she shielded her child against the attack of the flying beasts. Wentworth whipped open the door, felt the wind snatch it from his hand and slam it back against the body of the car.

"This way!" he shouted. "This way! I'll save you!"

The woman cried out in joy and ran with increased speed toward the braking Daimler. Once let her get inside… Wentworth's automatics were in his hands. If he could only spot the bat that menaced her. Ah, a glimpse of a fluttering black form. The Spider's automatic blasted, hammered a bat into extinction. The woman was running toward him eagerly. She lifted her face, held the child out from her body in an effort to get it first into the protection of the car.

IT HAPPENED in a heartbeat of time. Before the woman's face, a black shadow flitted. Leathery wings covered the baby's head. Wentworth could not shoot. He sprang forward and another of the loathsome black things flicked out of the darkness. The woman's scream rose high, higher, shrilling terribly. She stopped and stood rigidly, arms lifting the baby high. Its cries had ceased now and abruptly her own scream strangled into nothingness. She crumpled to the pavement while the Spider was still ten feet away.

As if it echoed her dying scream, another cry broke out. It was shrill, wailing and it ached downward from the heavens. It rose, wavering, to a crescendo that made the cold flesh creep along Wentworth's spine, then died into a minor note that was like a death sob. The Spider shouted a curse. He knew that sound.

It had heralded the death of those score of men in Latham's mansion. Hearing it, Latham had cried, "Oh, God, the Bat Man."

The Bat Man! Wentworth's eyes quested upward toward the muggy skies that threw back glare of street lights. Instinctively, he flinched. A bat dodged at his face and Wentworth's gun blasted upward deafeningly. The beast was hurled upward by the impact of lead, thudded softly to the pavement. The air was suddenly full of them, dodging, diving, sweeping on the Spider. His guns spoke deliberately, with a fearful accuracy. Through the night once more rang the wailing, blood-chilling cry of the Bat Man.

"Master!" Ram Singh shouted. "Master, quickly come to cover. A cloud of bats!"

Wentworth darted toward the Daimler, while his eyes still searched the heavens. Nothing moved there for the space of a half-dozen seconds, then far up there where the lights just touched him, the Spider saw again the incredible image of the huge bat-like thing he had spotted against the moon when Latham had died—Good God, was it only a few hours ago?—Wentworth's twin guns spat a deadly hail upward toward that gliding figure. But he knew it was futile, knew even as he continued to smash lead upward until his guns were empty.

"Master!" Ram Singh screamed the warning this time.

Wentworth sprang toward the car. He felt a gentle touch on his shoulder and brushed frantically with a gloved hand, knocked off a vampire bat. Then he was inside and the door thudded shut behind him. He was not a moment too soon. A cloud of bats blotted out for an instant the street outside, fluttering past the closed window.

A shudder swept over the Spider's body. He was no coward. No man in the world could ever call him that. But the sight of those hundred deadly little beasts with their soft flight and their teeth whose kiss meant death shook him as no gunman's lead had ever done. The black cloud lifted and he saw that the body of the woman and the child was a moving, black mass of leather-winged creatures....

Beside him, June Calvert was sobbing, her face buried in her hands. Ram Singh was muttering harsh Hindustani curses under his breath. Up there where this dark side street intersected the brightness of Market, there was a sudden, dark rush of screaming people. Over their heads danced a myriad black, deadly forms, Wentworth's lips were motionless, thin against his teeth as he stuffed fresh clips of bullets into his automatics. He would do what he could, but in heaven's name, what could he accomplish with the slaughter of a few bats? Something like a groan of despair pushed its way out between his clenched teeth.

Up there in the heavens, that winged monster watched the work of his kindred fiends, the bats. And....

Once more came that wailing, mocking cry. Damn it, the Bat Man was laughing, *laughing...!*

CHAPTER 4
BAT MAN VS. SPIDER

R AM SINGH thrust the Daimler toward where the crowd milled and slapped the air to drive off the deadly bats. Wentworth beat his knees with clenched fists. His guns were so futile against the hundreds of flying things. There *must* be some other method of fighting against them…!

As the car rolled out into Market Street, men and women grabbed at the handles and sought to force their way inside. Wentworth had locked the doors. It was necessary if he were to accomplish anything at all. He might save a half-dozen persons inside the car, but that would keep him from work which might save hundreds… He saw a fire-alarm box on a corner and shouted sharply to Ram Singh to halt.

He sprang from the car, fought his way through the crowds. The bats hovered just overhead. Now and again, one would dart downward and a man or woman would scream and die. Wentworth wore gloves, as always when he was in the Spider's disguise, and now he dragged his long, black cape up over his head, tearing a hole through which he might look. Twice, he felt the feathery touch of a bat lighting upon tile cape and the hint of their poisonous death tightened his lips grimly. He reached the alarm box, jerked open the door and yanked the lever. If the firemen could smash through, there might be a chance….

Across the street a theater was gay with many-colored lights. Police stood behind the closed, glass doors, he saw. Despite his anger, Harrington had taken the Spider's advice. Perhaps a few hundreds who might otherwise die terribly would be saved as a result of that.

Wentworth dared not uncover his head, lest the bats strike at him and without better vision, he could not shoot. Still, he did not dare return to the car lest he not be able to give the firemen the only suggestion that he thought might help. If they put on smoke helmets and covered their hands, they would be virtually immune to the attack....

A crashing blast across the street pulled his startled gaze to the theater. He heard the crash again and saw one of the inner doors crash outward, saw an axe glitter coldly. Even as the police whirled with their nightsticks ready, other doors crashed outward and the entire audience of the theater came streaming out into the street.

"Bats!" a man screamed. "The theater is full of bats!"

Wentworth saw a woman attempting to cover her bare shoulders with a cape, saw a bat settle like a loathsome, black flower upon her bosom. The woman fell. He started across the street, but a new rush of terrified men and women drove him back. The hoarse sirens of the fire engines cut through the medley of terror and pain. The trucks were literally ploughing their way through the crowds. Wentworth saw that the men already had donned their smoke helmets. He nodded approval. If he could find the man who had ordered that, he wouldn't have any trouble putting over his idea....

A battalion-chief's car jangled its way through solid ranks of screaming, dying people and the chief sprang out. He dodged as a bat flitted at him, ducked back inside the car and put on a smoke helmet. Wentworth rushed to his side, spat out his idea in swift words.

"Get hoses going," he shouted. "Knock people down and keep the streams going above them. Bats can't get through."

The battalion-chief was a gray-haired man. Wentworth saw his shrewd, smoke-narrowed eyes through the goggle eyes of the helmet. The driver of the car was rigid with fear, fear of the bats, fear of the man whose face he glimpsed when Wentworth lifted the hood of his cape. The chief nodded. He took off the smoke helmet long enough to shout orders. Wentworth dashed back to his car, ducked inside and began shooting.

"Get in front," he ordered June Calvert. "In front, but leave the glass slide open."

THE GIRL hesitated, then clambered over the back of the seat. There were two panes of glass that slid in grooves between front and rear of the car. She left one open. Wentworth took off his hat, then flung open one door of the car. For long, dreadful seconds nothing happened, then a bat flicked into the interior, dropped toward Wentworth's face. He swept his hat swiftly up and knocked the bat to the seat. It would be helpless there. Bats have no way of taking off from a horizontal surface. They cannot take off from a porch which is less than several feet from the floor, for a bat takes off by dropping free, spreading its wings, then gliding. With its wings already spread, it might take off from a lower object, but the seat would not permit that. Wentworth waited, his hat poised, his split second muscles set for the perilous task of capturing bats whose merest bite would be fatal.

One hose already was hissing out its stream of water into the crowd of Market Street. Men and women were bowled over and bats were washed out of the air to flutter helplessly on the pavement. Given time, they might work their way up the side of some building and fly again, but they would be given no opportunity for that.

Time after time, Wentworth's hat swept a bat from mid-flight to the seat and finally he slammed the door, crawled into the front section of the car and closed the glass slide. He sat looking over the water-flooded street. Many of the crowd had caught the idea of the hoses—a dozen were operating now and were throwing themselves down beneath the protecting streams. The battalion-chief had evidently sent in a call for more trucks for the hoarse cry of their sirens filled the air.

Crowds were streaming now from every theater with cries that they were filled with bats. Wentworth's heart was heavy within him. It had been at his order that people had been kept prisoner in those theaters. Harrington would be glad to give the excuse that the Spider had advised the action. He could hear the man's grandiloquent voice now.

"Gentleman of the press, you all know what the Spider has done for us in the past. I thought him an honorable man, fighting for the law in his own peculiar way. Naturally when he advised a thing, I considered it seriously. Hold the people in the theaters—yes, it seemed a good idea. How could I know that the Spider had turned into a mad dog who should be exterminated on sight? I have given my men orders to that effect. To shoot the Spider on sight...."

Yes, Harrington would talk like that. The Spider had tried to serve and he had led the people he sought to protect into a trap for the Bat Man. Regardless of whether he had convinced June Calvert, her earlier testimony that she had seen the Spider carrying a cage of bats would be revived. Wentworth laughed grimly. It only made his task more difficult. He closed his eyes, pressed them with heavy fingers. There was so much death, so much tragedy all about. What, in heaven's name, could be the purpose behind this wholesale slaughter of the innocents? If only he could have foreseen what was happening, have had Nita here earlier....

Wentworth pulled up his head. There was work to do. Not yet had the Bat Man called home his charges with that thin, gigantic squeaking... He turned to Ram Singh.

"I must thank you for standing by the Spider in time of trouble," he said crisply. "Many men would have fled from the scene of disaster the moment a gun was taken away from their back. You must tell me your master's name that I may commend you to him. Meantime, get us away from here at once. Miss Calvert, I am sure that soon it will be safe to go abroad. I am going to put you in the protection of some building...."

WENTWORTH'S WORDS cut off as he met the black, blazing regard of her eyes. There was hatred there, more than suspicion, certainty. Good lord! Had she penetrated his subter-

Above him, within pistol range, was the

huge creature he had seen twice before!

fuge with Ram Singh? Had she detected the fact that they worked together, that the Hindu was in reality the servant of the Spider! If she had....

"You, you fiend!" she choked. "You almost tricked me. But it was *you* who kept those people in the theaters so that the bats could kill them. You are the Bat Man, and...."

Wentworth shrugged, motioned to Ram Singh and the great car purred away from the spot where the dead lay in the streets beside the panicked living who crouched beneath the protection of the fire hoses. June Calvert ceased to talk and only glared at him angrily. Luckily, she had no gun... She was put out presently at the entrance of a subway that would shelter her from bats. Wentworth spun to Ram Singh.

"Find me a taxi immediately," he said sharply. When the Daimler surged forward, Wentworth rapidly instructed the Hindu in the course he must follow. Moments later, the Spider, stripped of cape and hat, part of the disguise removed from his face, sprang into a cab.

"Fifty dollars if you make the airport in twenty minutes," he ordered. "Ten more for every minute you shave off of that."

The taxi's forward lurch hurled him back against the cushions and he eased to a more comfortable position, drew out cigarettes and lighter. If only the Bat Man would delay for a while his signal to the bat horde... He shook his head. There was small hope of that. Already the attack must have lasted for over half an hour, the hungry bats were becoming sated. Probably he would have no such luck.

The motor of the cab snarled with speed. They shot over

the bridge toward Camden and the hiss of the wind increased. Wentworth had not doubted that Ram Singh would do his part. He had known just where to send the Hindu for the materials needed… The Spider's mind was weary with futile contemplation of the tragedy he had seen, the hundreds laid in writhing death in the streets. He had certain lines of investigation he could start. That spear which had been hurled through the window of Latham's home. He had noticed certain of its characteristics and was pretty certain that it was of a type used by the headhunters of the extreme reaches of the Amazon, the Jivaro Indians. A ridiculous idea, that those fiercely independent Indians could have been brought to America, or could have come of their own accord. But then it was ridiculous, too, that vampire bats had invaded the temperate zones. Neither seemed possible… yet hundreds had died of their poisoned bite this night. Yes, literally hundreds. He glanced at his watch, then out at the dark buildings streaking past. The taxi was making good time.

Finally the lights of the airport came in view. The driver slammed up to the administration building, twisted about to blink behind horn-rimmed spectacles.

"I think you will find the exact time about seventeen minutes, sir," he said in polite, precise English.

Wentworth tossed him a hundred dollar bill and raced toward the main building. He glimpsed a low-winged monoplane on the tarmac of a nearby hangar, its motor ticking over and swerved in his race. Minutes were precious, terribly precious. It was barely possible that the Bat Man had not yet sounded the

recall for the bats. Even if he had, swift action might yet win the day for the Spider....

WENTWORTH REACHED the plane in a pounding sprint. A mechanic stood with a pilot at the door of the hangar and they turned in amazement at sight of the running figure. Something of his purpose they must have guessed, but not in time to accomplish anything. Even as they started forward, shouting, Wentworth toed the wing, sprang to the cockpit and instantly yanked the throttle wide. The plane's engine spluttered, then bellowed. The ship began to trundle down the tarmac. It was a Lockhead, a type with which Wentworth was entirely familiar. He jockeyed to gain speed rapidly. For seconds, there was danger that the pursuing pair could reach the tail and nail it to the ground. Then the ship gathered way. An air-liner was

circling the field for a landing and the operations officer atop the administration building's coning tower flicked a red light at Wentworth frantically. The Spider glanced aloft, gauged his distances and sent his powerful monoplane off the ground downwind.

For seconds, the ship climbed sluggishly, then its speed picked up and he sent it racing at low altitude toward Philadelphia. He could not have wished for a better plane, but he longed for the machine guns of his scarlet Northrup. No way of knowing into what peril he flew tonight.

The lights of Philadelphia sprang at him. Within minutes, he was circling over its streets, peering down into the canyons and seeking the square to which he had directed Ram Singh. It was difficult at night, but after five minutes of circling, he located the place. His altitude was no more than four hundred feet. He drew an automatic and fired two shots. Staring down at the Square, he saw the flashes of Ram Singh's answering gun.

Suspenseful moments passed then while Wentworth hung the Lockhead in the sky, watching, watching… His panted breath of relief was almost a triumphant shout when, against the blackness of the square, he caught a dozen flitting bats which glowed as with phosphorescence. Ram Singh had succeeded then, had obtained the radiolite paint and sprayed the vampire bats with it, afterward providing them perches so that they could wing from the Daimler at the proper time. Now, if the Spider could keep them in sight and follow them to whatever place they had been kept, it was likely the Bat Man would not be far away!

At first, the glowing spots that were the bats flew about in seeming bewilderment, then they turned westward and, grouped loosely together, flew steadily in a straight course. Three times, the bats turned from their steady flight and each time a man in the streets died beneath their teeth. Wentworth, circling grim-lipped in the heavens, saw, and could do nothing. But he swore a hard oath that the Bat Man and his followers should pay for each of these lives. They were martyrs to the cause of justice....

Finally, the last of the houses of Philadelphia was gone from under Wentworth and still the bats winged on into the darkness. It was easier to follow them since the city lights no longer blinded him. It was necessary for him to swing in tight circles. The bats flew much more slowly than the plane, yet if he swung wide he might very well lose sight of their glowing bodies.

The flight moved on and on westward. Wentworth almost despaired of any definite goal for the bats. It seemed impossible that they should have been released so far from the city and yet sweep so directly there. Yet they flew fairly close together and bats generally traveled in pairs at most, generally alone. There must be some reason for this group migration....

SUDDENLY, THROUGH the vibration of the plane's motor, Wentworth heard a shrill, wailing note that he recognized instantly. It was followed immediately by the squeaking rasp, as of a giant bat. The glowing flight below him faltered in its steady progression. He realized that they were no longer pushing forward, but were climbing straight toward him!

It was impossible. No one could so direct and guide bats, and yet—and yet here they came directly toward his swift plane! The answer came to him almost with the realization of their

59

approach. The shrill squeak of the giant bat had come *from his direction!* The bats only flew toward the sound, then—then....

With a cold chill of apprehension racing up his spine, Wentworth tilted back his head to stare upward into the heavens. Then he kicked the rudder violently. The Lockhead rocked, spun to the left and Wentworth snapped a gun into his hand, staring with incredulous eyes at the black shadow that had seemed to float above him in the heavens.

Above him, almost within pistol range, was the huge creature that he had seen twice now upon the scene of vampire murder. Even as Wentworth spotted the thing, he saw flame streak from somewhere near its head and a rifle bullet cracked past his head!

An oath squeezed out between the Spider's locked teeth. No longer was there any doubt the thing was human. It might have wings, might skim the skies like a bat, but it was human. No bat could fire a rifle. With the thought, Wentworth yanked back the stick and drove straight at the thing, automatic ready in his hand....

Once more the rifle cracked and the bullet dug into the fuselage beside Wentworth's shoulder. The Spider kicked the rudder, skidding the plane about. He was within range now and the Spider's lead never missed.... His automatic was ready, but its muzzle swept empty air! In the instant it had taken Wentworth's plane to wheel about, the Bat Man—it could be no other—had disappeared! Even as he made that discovery, lead whistled upward past his gun hand.

The Spider's lips twisted against his teeth. He shoved the stick against the instrument panel and the Lockhead dropped her nose like a plummet. In a heartbeat, he had lost two hundred feet. But he had not caught the Bat Man. He had a glimpse of him in the instant the ship's nose had gone down. The Bat Man had stood on his tail for that shot upward at the ship and as Wentworth swept by, he was in the midst of a whipstall....

As the phrase *whipstall* snapped through Wentworth's brain, he gasped. Gasped even as he threw two swift shots at the Bat Man. There was time for no more. He was dangerously close to the ground and the Lockhead was heavy, its wing spread proportionally small. Down, down she went while he maneuvered rudder and aerolons. The Lockhead came out of it with twenty-five feet to spare. Wentworth zoomed, *viraged* to spot the Bat Man... He was gone! As quickly as that, in the few seconds while the Lockhead dived for earth and zoomed out of it, the flying man had vanished.

Wentworth eagerly scanned the earth below, but there was nothing there, no movement, no sound—and no place where a plane might land even if the Bat Man were down there. Sudden wild hope sang through Wentworth's brain. Had those two swift shots, thrown in the midst of a power dive of terrific speed, knocked down the Bat Man? Slowly, the Spider shook his head. It was barely possible, but even his extraordinary aim would scarcely be equal to that task. Besides, he was certain that his zoom, his *virage* would have been quick enough to spot a Bat Man tumbling to earth. However, if he had dived....

Wentworth's mind turned back to the idea that had flashed through his brain as he had darted past the Bat Man. *Whipstall!* That described the performance of the winged man. It was a phrase applied to planes that, rising too steeply, slapped straight down to the ground as if the tail were the handle of a whip and the nose the lash. A bird couldn't perform an operation such as that if it wished, nor could a bat.

To Wentworth that meant only one thing. That Bat Man was an ordinary human being... *with wings attached to his body like a plane!* As the idea struck, a memory came to the Spider. Recently, at Miami, a "daredevil" had dropped from a plane with triangular canvas wings stretching from arms to his body and another fin between his legs. With their aid, he had looped and stunted in the air, finally using a parachute to land. Why wouldn't it be possible, by extending those wings to each side with struts and braces, to operate precisely as a motorless glider?

By the gods, the thing sounded possible! There was no time now, of course, to figure weight per square foot, gliding angles... While he thought, Wentworth had been scouring the country below him, hoping against hope that he might catch some glimpse of the blowing bats. But it was in vain. The Bat Man had accomplished his purpose. He had almost killed Wentworth with his rifle, operated in what way God only knew, and he had distracted him until the murdering bats could escape.

Spider and Bat Man had met—and it was the Bat Man who had won!

CHAPTER 5
DINNER WITH DEATH

WEARILY, WENTWORTH turned the Lockhead back toward Camden airport. Undoubtedly all fields had been warned to watch out for a stolen ship. He smiled slightly, took the stick between his knees and stripped off the remnants of his disguise. Many things could be forgiven Richard Wentworth, especially if he paid well....

He had no more trouble on landing than he had anticipated and found Ram Singh waiting for him with the Daimler. He settled gratefully into the cushions. A half hour later he was asleep at his rooms in the Early Quaker, an ancient and quiet hotel on the waterfront. He was astir early, found a note on his bedside table that Nita van Sloan already had arrived in response to his summons. A smile touched his lips. He lifted the note, in Nita's own handwriting, to his lips, and crossed to the telephone, got her rooms at once.

"Darling," he cried jubilantly, "could you find it in your heart to have breakfast with me, oh practically at once?"

"I thought the invitation was for dinner," she told him, "but it's just possible that I'm not engaged...."

It was pleasant in the informal dining room of the Early Quaker. Its flooring was the ancient boards of a wharf and extended out over the river. Mooring rungs were still fastened there, and there was always the pleasant suck and murmur of the tide among the piles. The wharf had been glassed in and, open now, allowed the warm, morning sunlight to stream through.

Nita's smile, as Wentworth greeted her in the lobby, was warm and welcoming. Her violet eyes were deep and the bronze-lit curls that clustered about the perfect oval of her face were incredibly lovely. Wentworth told her so in a soft murmur as he took her arm and led her toward the sunlit dining room. Nita's lips were curved in a remembering smile. Their pleasurable moments together were all too brief. Greatly they loved, but the Spider could never marry. How could a man take on the responsibilities of wife and children when any moment might find the disgracing hand of the law upon his shoulder—when any night might bring his death at the hands of one of a hundred enemies?

No, Wentworth had sacrificed his hope of personal happiness for the sake of the thousands of others who would be denied peace, perhaps even life, if the arch criminals that now and again arose, were not put down by the Spider. He had never regretted his choice, but there were times when bitterness touched his soul....

At a table where they could gaze out on the blue of the Delaware River, Nita touched Wentworth's hand, her violet eyes gravely on his.

"I see that they blame the Spider again," she said.

Wentworth shrugged. "It is inevitable, I suppose. How do the newspapers explain the Spider's calling fire engines and directing the firemen to save the people with their hoses?"

Nita glanced toward the approaching waiter. "They don't explain it. Dick. They don't mention it at all."

Wentworth grimaced. The battalion-chief, then, had taken credit for the idea. Well, it did not matter. He began to tell Nita the events of the night before. He had no secrets from her. Often she helped him in his battles and more than once she had herself worn the Spider's mantle, and made the Spider's kills....

The day passed without further event and Wentworth spent the time conferring with police officials, seeking some clue to the reason behind the wholesale slaughters of the Bat Man. He found no motive, but he learned one thing that made his lips thin with determination. The Crosswinds Jockey club was holding an annual banquet at the Early Quaker this evening.

It was a quasi-social affair and he decided at once to attend. Even though the Bat Man had been striking at random at humanity, it seemed likely he would still follow the aim of his first attacks—the race track. Even if there were no new assault, it was possible that Wentworth might pick up some lead to the killer. Certainly, the man must be some one familiar with racing and the coterie connected with it. He might very well still be associated with the turf himself....

AN INVITATION was easy to arrange and the dinner he had planned with Nita was shared with some hundred other persons, social celebrities and turf men. Commissioner of Police Harrington was there at the head table with Wentworth and Nita. His red-jowled face was far from pleasant. It was plain that the overwhelming tragedies of the last twenty-four hours weighed heavily upon him.

Wentworth had scarcely seated Nita when a blond, handsome man who towered even above Wentworth's six feet came eagerly to them.

"I say!" he cried. "Aren't you Nitita—I'm sorry—Nita van Sloan?"

Nita looked up questioningly then sprang to her feet and held out both hands.

"Piggy!" she cried. "Piggy Stoking. In heaven's name…!"

Wentworth stood politely by, smiling slightly, estimating the taper-shouldered strength of the man, taking in the youthful but determined face. Nita turned toward Wentworth, flushed a little.

"This is Frederick Stoking, who was my first beau," she told him, laughing. "He used to pull my pigtails when… when I wore pigtails. Richard Wentworth, Fred."

The two men bowed, shaking hands, taking each other's measure. Wentworth decided Stoking was intelligent, and steady, just as his wide-set, blue eyes were. There was a deep cleft in a firm chin. Without consciously willing it, he compared himself and this man who had been Nita's first beau. They were very much of an age, he and Stoking, but the trials he had undergone, the woes and the pains, had taken their toll of Wentworth's face. There were lines at his mouth corners, a sharpness to his nose. Stoking was gay.

"You must join us after the banquet." Wentworth said cordially. "I'd like very much to hear about Nita's pigtails."

Stoking's eyes were grave despite the laughter about his mouth. "They were just as lovely as her curls are now," he said. "I pulled them, but I assure you it was reverently."

Nita laughed at him. "None the less painfully!"

Stoking left and Wentworth and Nita both watched his superb figure as he moved back to his own party. Wentworth

Rays of light shone from above on the men who had released the bats!

looked down at his plate, reflecting a score of yellow lights. His mouth was unconsciously grim. He was not thinking anything definitely, but there was a darkness, a depression, of his spirits.

Nita's hand touched his arm. "Why, Dick!" She whispered. "I do believe you're jealous!"

Wentworth straightened his shoulders, put a smile on his lips, but he spoke very quietly. "Darling, I am jealous for the normal happiness that might have been yours if you had never met me. Why should you be burdened down, as I am, with the cares of the world?"

Nita's hand tightened on his arm. "If you don't stop that, I shall kiss you right here in public," she said fiercely. "Perhaps I prefer to be burdened."

Wentworth laughed, patted her hand, and shrugged aside his depression. He leaned toward Nita, named all the celebrities present. "I am suspicious of all small men," he told her. "There's that jockey over there at the third table. An ex-jockey, rather, turned stables owner. He's very successful and bats haven't killed any of his horses. Sanderson is the name. He still doesn't weigh above ninety pounds."

"Why small men?" Nita asked.

"I've estimated the wing spread of the Bat Man, gliding angles, weight per square foot. He couldn't perform in the air as he does with that wing spread and weigh much over a hundred pounds. For instance, the man next to him, another ex-jockey named Earl Westfall, couldn't possibly manage himself on the wings. He's put on a lot of weight for his height, must weigh about a hundred and eighty to judge from his girth."

NITA'S HAND still clung to his arm. She tightened her fingers. "That redheaded man bending over Commissioner Harrington's shoulder...?"

"Red Cullihane," Wentworth said briefly. "Partner of Latham, who was killed last night." He felt a tingling race over his body as he studied the stubby, powerful build of the man, a tingling of apprehension. Cullihane's presence here spelled danger for all of them. Suppose the Bat Man should strike at him tonight, at this banquet? If the man's intention was merely promiscuous slaughter, the gathering here offered an excellent opportunity, especially if people connected with the turf were still mainly his targets. Wentworth's eyes tightened, his hands beneath the table clenched into hard knots. He was suddenly sure that his premonition was correct, that there would be slaughter here tonight....

He glanced swiftly about the banquet hall, built out over the Delaware River on piles, an ancient wharf actually. The glassed sides were open wide and through them now and then came the moan of a tug whistle, but there were tight-fitted screens. They could be smashed out by the same means that had been used at Latham's home, but Wentworth doubted that method. It would allow too slow ingress for the number of bats necessary to dispose of the entire gathering... Nevertheless, he was certain that the attack would take place.

Wentworth's smile tightened, thinned his lips. Queer, these premonitions of his. They were rarely wrong and he had come to believe them to be based on the intuitive workings of his subconscious mind. He no longer strove to trace out the reasons, merely accepted the conclusion thus presented to him. There would be an attack here tonight.

Somehow, his mind refused to apply itself to the problem of defense. There was no reason for the lethargy. He was thoroughly rested after the strenuous activities of the previous twenty-four hours. Yet, instead of planning strategy, he found himself gazing time and again at the man who had been Nita's first beau. Fred Stoking's eyes kept straying toward Nita, too.

Nita's hand touched Wentworth's arm. "What's the matter, Dick boy?" she whispered.

There wasn't anything the matter, except that he felt a vast reluctance for the encounter that was approaching. Good God, would there never be an end of this ceaseless fighting?—Never an end of the warped madmen who sought nation-wide dominion through crime? He knew a strange rebellion that he, and he alone, should meet these terrors....

"Nita," he spoke abruptly, "I want you to join Stoking's party and get them to leave here at once on some pretext."

Nita's fingers tightened on his arm. "What is it?"

"There's going to be a bat attack here," he told her, barely breathing the words. "I know it, but I couldn't persuade anyone to believe me. I don't even wish to prevent it. If I don't permit the attack, I won't be able to trail the Bat Man."

Nita started to protest, but a glimpse of Wentworth's bitter eyes stopped the words on her lips. She looked at him a bit curiously. His desire to remove her from the path of danger was understandable enough, but why Piggy Stoking?

Wentworth smiled at her slightly, reading the question in her eyes. "I rather like the lad," he said. "Besides I want to check up on your past and if he were killed, I couldn't do it."

HE ROSE to his feet and Nita, perforce, stood also. She looked up into the lean, tanned face she loved, the smile fading from her lips. So often, so often they had parted like this on the eve of peril and death....

"Be careful, Dick!"

"For you, sweetheart!"

Many eyes followed Nita and Wentworth as they crossed the floor to Stoking's table. They made a brave couple, those two, alike in proud carriage, with that touch of arrogance in the poise of the head, confidence like an accolade upon their shoulders.

"I'm called away unexpectedly," Wentworth told Stoking. "I'm sure I can trust you since there are no pigtails to pull."

"I make no promises," Stoking warned him. "Those curls tempt me, too."

Wentworth bowed his way from the table, his smile lingering mechanically on his lips. From the antechamber, he sent for Commissioner Harrington. The man came heavily toward him, shorter than Wentworth, a frown between his eyes.

"What's up?" he asked crisply.

Wentworth's face was as grave as his. "Bats," he said "At least seventy-five per cent of the guests tonight are associated with the race track. They got Latham. Cullihane, with whom Latham was associated, is present."

Harrington tried to laugh it off. "You're of the belief then, that these attacks are sponsored by some crooks or another? You believe in this Bat Man?"

Quick anger throbbed ever Wentworth. It was the unbelief of men like this, the slowness of authorities entrusted with the protection of humanity, that necessitated the activities of the Spider. Oh, for the keen strength of Governor Kirkpatrick in a time like this! Kirk, who had been police commissioner of New York City for years, had never hesitated....

"Very well," Wentworth told Harrington coldly, "Doubt me and watch your friends die." He turned on his heel and strode away.

Commissioner Harrington came after him hurriedly. "No offense intended, Wentworth," he said. "Surely, you must realize it's hard to believe in a man with wings...."

Wentworth turned toward him. "It's no man with wings," he said shortly. "But a man who has rigged a bat-like glider. You've heard of motorless gliders, haven't you? I fought with him last night and he outmaneuvered me. Naturally, the shorter the wingspread, and axis, the more quickly the craft can pivot or dodge." He recounted briefly his battle with the Bat Man the night before. He stopped once to bow as Nita and the Stoking party passed them. His eyes saluted Nita for her achievement, then he turned back to Harrington and continued his story. When he had finished, the Commissioner frowned heavily, staring at the floor, standing with braced legs hands locked behind his back.

"I cannot doubt you," he said. "I know what you've done in New York, of course, against criminals. You must pardon my hesitation. The conception is a bit bizarre."

Wentworth acknowledged that with a short nod. "Quite, but

I do not make statements unless I have ample reason for them. I tell you that the bats will attack here tonight. I do not know when, but...."

His words broke off as a piercing wail, a sobbing moan swelled into the antechamber where the two men stood.

"The Bat Man!" Wentworth rasped.

As if his words bad been a signal, the lights blinked out and a deathly stillness fell upon the gabble of the banquet hall, upon the entire hotel. Then a woman screamed.

"The bats!" she cried, and a panic roar followed her scream.

Wentworth's hand closed on Harrington's arm. He felt the man's start at his touch. "Perhaps next time," Wentworth shouted at him, "you *will* believe!"

CHAPTER 6
WATERS OF DOOM

WENTWORTH'S FACE was grimly set as he raced to the battle against the poisonous bats. If only he had begun earlier his attempt to persuade Harrington! But it was useless to reproach himself. He had acted immediately after the discovery of what impended. Only one thing to do now: attempt to save the lives of these trapped banqueters.

He fled headlong for the outer door and as he reached the curb, the long, low form of his Daimler rolled forward, jerked to a halt. He snapped open the back door, reached inside and snatched out a large drum-like object of glittering chromium. As he started back for the door of the hotel again, the driver sprang to the street and reached his side in long strides.

"Stay here, Ram Singh," Wentworth ordered. "Throw the switch as soon as I get inside."

The turbaned Hindu scowled at being barred from the battle, but there was no hesitation in his movements. He leaped back into the car. Wentworth shouldered open the doors of the hotel and instantly a wide beam of light blazed out from the drum-like object he carried. He hurried with it to the door of the banquet hall and its powerful ray illuminated the entire room.

The air was filled with the fluttering small messengers of death and streams of them poured upward through traps opened in the floor, Wentworth cursed. He should have seen that method of attack. The wharf floor had been preserved in its original form. "Atmosphere" for the hotel. The Bat Man had merely opened the trap doors that once had been used by workmen and released his hordes of killers. Wentworth thanked the gods for his foresight in putting the powerful searchlight into the car. He had not expected this attack tonight, but had prepared for future frays. Now the blazing white beam was blinding the bats. Many of them were fluttering back into the pits from which they rose, while others swung blindly about the room in their heavy, laborious flight. Two score of men and women lay upon the floor, dead from the bites of the starved vampires—but the light had saved a hundred others!

Wentworth did not delay on the scene after placing the light. A single glance had pictured the hall indelibly upon his mind, then he turned and raced for the outer doors again. It would be impossible, he knew, to attack from here the men who had brought the bats. It would be certain death to attempt to descend through those bat-crowded trap-doors. But there was another way....

As he sprang to the street he saw Ram Singh's knife glittering in the air. Four men were trying to slice the cable that fed current to the searchlight. Wentworth' twin automatics flew to his hands. He shot twice. Ram Singh's blade had disposed of the other two. His teeth flashed white in a smile as he faced his master.

"My knife is thirsty, master," he cried in Hindustani. "It has but sipped a drop or two...!"

Wentworth had not paused while he shot. Now he thrust his guns back into their holsters and, with a gesture to the Hindu, raced for a wharf from which he could reach the river. Ram Singh loped along beside him. He was chanting under his breath, a war song in which the exploits of his wonderful knife figured large.

A high board fence bordered the wharf. Wentworth sprang upward and seized its top. Instantly, Ram Singh caught his feet and helped him. Straddling the top, Wentworth reached down a hand to the Hindu. Below him the water was black with wavering white shadows of lights upon its surface. Under the piles which supported the dining room of the Early Quaker were only shadows....

Wentworth stripped off coat and shoes. He thrust his automatics into Ram Singh's hands.

"Thy knife, warrior!" he ordered.

THE SPIDER

RAM SINGH wiped the blade across his thigh and Wentworth gripped it between his teeth, dived into the black water. There was scarcely a splash to mark his smooth entrance. Ripples spread quietly and lapped against the piles, making zig-zags of the light's reflections. But Wentworth's head did not break the surface again. Under water, he stroked for the darkness beneath the Quaker wharf. Under there somewhere were the men of the Bat Master, loosing' new killers upon the people above.

When he rose to the surface, it was with his fingers against the barnacle-studded base of a pile. His head lifted without a sound and he peered, narrow-eyed, through the darkness. Rays of light escaped from the banquet hall overhead. By that faint illumination, Wentworth made out the shadows of four boats. In each a man crouched beside a high cage from which the bats had been released. Even as he spotted them, the boats began to ease away from the trapdoors.

Noiselessly, Wentworth stroked toward the nearest. As he approached, the man in it slid over the side and vanished into the black water. Wentworth whipped the knife from between his teeth and dived. It was not the kind of weapon he liked, but this was no time for niceties. This man in the water was a knife at his back, a threat of death. What Wentworth sought was a live prisoner, but this swimming assassin….

There could be no vision under this black surface, but Wentworth had marked the other's course and his knife fist groped before him. He touched living flesh, felt it flinch away and stroked mightily forward at the same time lunging with the knife as with a sword. Its keen point bit deep. He wrenched free and struck twice more, then swept backwards. There was a great, kicking commotion that made the water boil. The dying man's head breached and Wentworth heard a gasped cry in a language he did not recognize. Instantly the other three men took to water… diving toward the Spider!

Wentworth stroked softly away from the spot where his victim had sunk. He must fight this out in the water for the air was filled with a soft fluttering of bats, and their hungry squeaking. He glimpsed one against the faint light from above and dodged beneath the surface as it fluttered toward him. His lips shut in a thin line, his eyes narrowed against the darkness. Death above from the fangs of a myriad bats; and in the water, death at the hands of three men whose companion he had killed. If only he had his automatics, dry and ready for action! But he had only Ram Singh's knife. A round head broke water within a yard of his face….

On the instant, Wentworth flung himself toward it, his knife flashing in a cutting swing. The head flinched back out of range and instantly disappeared. But not before Wentworth had caught a glimpse of a knife between its teeth, a knife that now would be reaching for his groin!

Useless to try to flounder backward out of range. The knife-man would have the speed of a dive behind him. Wentworth did the only possible thing. He plunged forward and to one side at the same time. He had a glimpse of two other men moving toward him, then he pivoted to strike at his immediate assailant. The man's knife broke water first, thrusting toward the spot where a moment before Wentworth had been.

WENTWORTH DID not wait for the whole man to show, but dived with the knife pointed for the body behind that arm. This time he felt his knife bite home. He did not attempt a second stroke, but swept on past the man, dragging his knife with him. Deadly blind work, this fighting in black water beneath a black, wooden roof. No telling where the knife had struck but no death flurry threshed the water above his head....

Wentworth stroked cautiously beneath the water, knife hand feeling ahead for obstructions. He touched the shell-roughened surface of a pile, circled it and allowed himself to drift upward. His lungs were bursting; there was a heavy heart-pound in his ears. But when his head eased above the surface, he dared not let the air escape rapidly. Behind his post, he waited, listening as the humming in his ears subsided.

Not a sound broke the silence save the squeaking of the bats. Up there in the banquet hall was silence, too. But Wentworth did not push out into the open. Probably the two, or possibly three, men left were doing as he was, clinging to piles and waiting for the enemy to betray himself. Well, the Spider still had a stratagem in reserve. Without a sound, he submerged and swam toward the spot where he had entered under the wharf.

It was laborious work. He dared not dive, lest the splashing betray him. He must waste precious time submerging, pushing off from the base of a pile and groping ahead lest he ram head-on into another. Twice he submerged before, in the dimness, he could detect open space ahead of him. Then he exhaled loudly, began to swim with small, secret splashings, deliberately making noise. Behind him all was silence.

He swam on, not too swiftly. He gasped out words in Hindustani that sounded like curses of despair to his pursuers. He ordered Ram Singh to shoot when the men appeared, yet spare one. When he had gone fifty yards from the edge of the wharf, he peered behind him. With the speed of fish, two men were swimming after him. He began to flounder, as if helpless with fatigue. The knives in the mouths of his pursuers were visible now, glints of steel. But only two… Well, then, his knife thrust had gone home.

From the top of the fence, Ram Singh's automatic spat red flame. There was a thin, inarticulate cry and one of the heads vanished. They had been very close to Wentworth and with the shot and cry he spun about and sped in a racing trudgeon toward the remaining man. The knifeman paused uncertainly, turned and began to swim back toward the wharf but at a pace that was markedly slow and burdened. Triumph shot through Wentworth. He changed to a powerful overhand so that he could watch his victim… and his sense of triumph lessened. Seconds before the man had been swimming swiftly, easily. Even fear could not so quickly destroy his speed….

The thought had only half-formed in Wentworth's mind when he dived to one side, stroking with all his strength. He felt the faint concussion of Ram Singh's second shot and burst above the surface to find a second knife man beating up the water in a death-flurry. The original swimmer was making better time now for the wharf. It was obvious that, even as Wentworth's glancing thought had told him, the fellow's floundering was part of a trap. He had led Wentworth on until his companion could dive under water and knife Wentworth from behind. Only the Spider's keen powers of observation and split-second action had saved him. His face was set, hard. He raced on after the man whose antics had so nearly trapped him....

The man's efforts were feeble again, a great deal of splashing and small progress. Wentworth overtook him speedily, but delayed just out of his reach. The man turned and hit out impotently with his knife. With a quick grab, Wentworth had his wrist. A wrench and the weapon was sinking to the bottom. But the battle was not so soon over. He did not wish to kill the man, nor to die himself. The other seemed too determined to drag him down, even at the cost of his own life.

As he lunged, Wentworth had a first clear glimpse of his features. He frowned in bewilderment even as the man reached out to seize him. The man was obviously an Indian, short of stature with a flattish face and black, heavy hair. But he had no time for speculation, for the Indian fastened upon him with arms and legs and they instantly sank below the surface.

Black water closed over them and they drifted lower and lower toward the bottom. Wentworth struggled desperately to free himself, to free even one arm, but the Indian clung with the strength of a madman, arms and legs wrapped about him, head buried under Wentworth's chin. Already, the Spider's lungs seemed squeezed with iron torture bands—already his blood was humming in his ears. Hope of capturing the man alive fled from him. It seemed possible now that he himself would not escape from this fight alive!

Colored lights danced in the blackness of the water and he

knew that they signified approaching unconsciousness. But unconsciousness here meant death for the Spider—destruction for many thousands of others from the onslaughts of the Indians and their murdering bats! The Indian's arms seemed to lock more tightly about him....

CHAPTER 7
POISONED AMBUSH

WENTWORTH, SUFFOCATING beneath the waters in the grip of the Indian, had only one recourse. The knife between his teeth. He could not free his arm to wield it, but the Indian's head was beneath his chin. Slowly, with a sense of timelessness and enormous effort, Wentworth began to twist his head to one side, to turn the point of the knife between his teeth toward the Indian's neck.

The noise of his own laboring heart was thunderous in his ears. His lungs strained, strained. He blew out a little breath through his nostrils to relieve them, but instantly they were paining again. And he twisted his head, squirmed it sideways so that the long blade of the knife turned downward. All thought was done with now. Consciousness was almost gone, but still Wentworth's will drove his head to that slow twisting motion.

He was conscious of no movement, either in his own body, nor that of the Indian.

They were resting on the slimy bottom of the river, but he did not know when they had touched there. With a final exhaustion of will, he achieved the position of head that he desired and jabbed downward with the knife. There was a pain in his neck, a stabbing brilliance of agony that made him think he had knifed himself instead of the Indian, then there was a vast, absorbing darkness....

Even through that blackness, he had a sensation of lifting upward, though it seemed the Indian's arms were still about him. Impossible to know how long that oppressive darkness lasted, but finally he was looking up into the face of Ram Singh. The Hindu grinned widely.

"By Siva, *sahib*," he cried, "nothing can kill thee!"

Wentworth thrust himself up and found that he was inside of his car, the windows closed while black things hovered against it, the vampire killers of the Bat Man.

"Thy servant dived to help thee, master," Ram Singh went on, "but did not find thee until thou arosest thyself.'

Wentworth took account of himself slowly. His brain came flashing back to full life ahead of his laggard body. He had succeeded then in puncturing the Indian's spine and relaxing his death grip. But even then, he would have drowned had it not been for the ever-vigilant Ram Singh.

"I'm afraid," he whispered, "that I lost thy knife, O warrior!"

Ram Singh held up the glistening blade. Wentworth was rapidly regaining his strength. His maneuver against the Bat Man had failed through the bravery of the monster's men Indians. He recalled suddenly the Jivaro spear which had been driven through the window of Latham's mansion. He fumbled a flask of brandy out of a pocket of the car, took a long swig.

Ram Singh, squatting on the floor, was busied rewinding his turban.

"Wah! Those demons of Kali!" he exclaimed. "Thy servant was forced to hide his face in his turban to keep the bats from feasting on his blood while he sat upon the fence."

The potent liquor revived Wentworth's body, made his heart beat strongly. He leaned forward to his radio, tuned it carefully. From it issued a series of musical monotones... Ram Singh ceased the wrapping of his turban and listened. Wentworth began to smile.

"Quickly, Ram Singh," he cried. "That is Jackson in the plane. I set him to keep watch above on a chance that the Bat Man would strike. Jackson has followed..." Wentworth stopped to catch the rhythmic beat of wireless signals: "... followed a plane from which the Bat Man dived. It is over New Jersey. Quickly, Ram Singh, by way of Trenton...."

RAM SINGH climbed over the front seat and dropped behind the wheel. Wentworth had seen at a glance that the lights blazed now in the Early Quaker hotel and he severed the cable that connected with the searchlight he had carried into the building. The Daimler was instantly in motion....

For a while Wentworth rested. When Ram Singh had reached Roosevelt highway and was racing through the outskirts of Philadelphia toward Trenton, he opened the wardrobe behind the seat and substituted dry clothing for his ruined evening clothes. He donned dark tweeds. When the time came, he would add cape and broad-brimmed black hat, alter his face... and the

Spider would step forth from the car in all his sinister fearful majesty....

The wireless signals from Jackson continued to drum on his ears, repeating the message first sent and giving the new positions of the plane. Even if Jackson did not trail the ship to a hiding place of the Bat Man, they might capture the pilot and learn something from him. If they found a headquarters for the Indians... Well, there would be a new battle.

It was like the Spider that he should press on this way while his body still had not recuperated from a struggle that had nearly cost his life.

Because he was tired, he urged Ram Singh to greater speed in the pursuit. He warned the Hindu that, since they hunted Jivaros, they must be on the watch for poisoned blow-gun darts.

"The Jivaros are headhunters," he explained. "They strip the skin from the skull, stuff it and smoke it down to about the size of a doll's head. If you don't want that turbaned skull of yours to be hung up at a Jivaro feast, be careful!"

Wentworth knew that Ram Singh was laughing....

The Daimler rolled past a deserted, darkened air field and at Wentworth's quick order, Ram Singh whirled the mighty car about and sent it toward the hangar. It was necessary to use guns, even when Wentworth offered to buy a plane, before the single man on guard there could be persuaded to part with a fast ship. Wentworth left a check and sent the plane rocketing through the night. The ship was equipped with radio and Wentworth flashed a message to Jackson, received his joyous response. The Bat Man's ship was still boring steadily northward....

Twenty minutes later, Jackson's wireless spluttered rapid signals: "Attacked by two ships with machine guns. Over Shrewesbury River near Red Bank. They're good and...."

Then silence, blankness in the dark night above New Jersey. Wentworth caught at the throttle, but the plane already was doing its best, blazing through the black sky with its motor revving at dangerous speed. The Spider's mouth was a hard, uncompromising slit. Had Jackson, brave Jackson, paid the penalty of all who fought side by side with the Spider? A price of pain and blood and death? The empty sky gave him no answer. He pictured Jackson flaming down into the shallows of the Shrewesbury. Jackson who had fought with him in France, who had saved his life; and had his own saved in turn, a dozen times upon the battlefields of earth and sky! Jackson was battling for his life, had perhaps crashed in flames...!

SECONDS DRAGGED into minutes, each of which saw three miles of dark countryside slip past beneath hissing wings. Finally the dark shimmer of the river showed on the horizon and beside it spurted a bright gout of flame. Wentworth leaned forward in the pilot's seat, but he could make out no details of the scene below, no trace of hostile ships in the sky. At long last, he was circling over the spot of fire. It was the wreckage of a plane, but it was impossible to tell whether it was the Northrup... Wentworth put the ship into a steep dive, circled and landed on the meadow by the light of the burning ship.

The Spider sat motionless in his plane, the motor just ticking over, and stared at the wreckage. It was a biplane as his Northrup was, but beyond that he could tell nothing. He climbed out of the cockpit and Ram Singh vaulted to the ground beside him. Slowly they made their way forward....

"Master," said Ram Singh, "you warned me beware of blow-gun darts."

At the words, Wentworth stopped short, a new thought striking him. Was this a trap? He had been so wrapped up in the idea of Jackson's battle, of his crash and death, that he had not paused to think of trickery. But now he threw swift, piercing glances into the shadows that ringed the plane's fire like waiting jackals at a kill.

"Thanks, Ram Singh," he said quietly.

He led the way even closer to the ship. Its structure greatly resembled a Northrup, but Wentworth could not be sure because of the smashing of structure by the crash. He became aware of automobile headlights speeding along a nearby road and turned heavily back to his own plane. They left the ring of dying red fire, stepped into the darkness, twice black now since their eyes were narrowed by the flame, and....

"Duck, major!"

Jackson's hearty deep voice rang out of the night somewhere. Even while a leap of joy convulsed his heart, Wentworth snatched Ram Singh's arm and pulled him to the ground with him.

"Roll," he shouted. "Roll toward the plane!"

Over his head, he saw tiny three-inch darts sail past. Off in the darkness, came the popping of blow guns, as if corks had been pulled from many bottles. As he and Ram Singh rolled desperately toward the ship, more of those butterfly harbingers of death buried their poison points in the earth beside them. Wentworth sprang to his feet and ran zig-zag toward the ship, snatched the throttle wide. Instantly a hurricane of wind whistled past him and Ram Singh stood beside him, hands locked on the wing. Wentworth had set the brakes, but with the propeller bellowing, the plane might get loose.

Leaning against the slip-stream, Wentworth pulled his automatics. He could no longer hear the popping of blowguns, but he could trace the course of the feather-light tiny arrows. He and Ram Singh were safe now, protected by the wind as by a sheet of steel, for the darts did not carry enough force, or weight, to penetrate that hurricane. Wentworth's guns began to speak rhythmically and screeches of pain came from the night. His heart beat joyous rhythm to his shots. He had thought Jackson dead and now he was restored. His lips moved grimly at each bullet he pumped into the darkness.

"Jackson," he called. "Come to the ship!"

"Coming!" Jackson's deep voice echoed, then he burst zig-zagging into the circle of light, crossed it and raced toward the ship. Wentworth's guns sought out the sources of the darts that flew for him and presently Jackson was beside him, his thick chest heaving from his run. He stood *stiffly* as the soldier he was, wide shoulders braced, broad face expressionless.

"Lost the Northrup, sir," he shouted above the roar of the propellers.

"Saved our lives!" Wentworth shouted back at him. "Into the plane, sergeant. Ram Singh, at the controls."

Ram Singh loosed his hold on the wing. The ship was quivering with the battle between propeller and brakes. Released, it bounded scarcely seventy-five feet before it lifted its nose toward the skies. Wentworth, crowded into the forward cockpit with Jackson, fitted on head-phones and handed a pair to the sergeant.

"Report," Wentworth ordered briefly.

"Yes, sir," said Jackson, his voice at attention even though he himself was seated. "You know how I picked up a plane and followed. Got here, two other ships laid for me. Plane I followed kept right on. Tried to follow and two ganged up on me. Shot out my radio. Incendiary bullets got gasoline. Bailed out and parachuted into river. Got to wreck in time to see them sneaking devils trying to ambush you."

"Planes go away?" Wentworth inquired.

"Think they landed, sir," Jackson responded. "Not in sight when parachute opened."

Wentworth peered overside and found that Ram Singh was circling slowly, recalled he had not ordered any particular destination. Even as he looked, lights flared out over a field and three ships scuttled through it and bolted into the air. Wentworth laughed. Useless to attempt to fight three planes, when those ships had machine guns and he had only his automatics. But there was another way. He leaned forward and tapped Ram Singh's shoulder, shook his fist toward the lighted field.

Ram Singh twisted about and showed his gleaming teeth. While he still looked, the ship dipped nose down for the earth, diving straight toward the three rising planes!

CHAPTER 8
TRIUMPH OF THE BAT!

THE FANTASTIC courage of that unarmed dive upon three machine-gun planes stupefied the pilots of the attacking ships for a space of seconds. They scattered from under the headlong plunge of the Spider's plane, breaking their formation, darting in all directions to escape what seemed a suicidal attack.

Wentworth's plane, under the steady hand of Ram Singh, flashed past them toward the field before they realized their mistake. When they whirled to the assault, it was almost too late. Ram Singh was floating in to a landing near the hangar at the upwind end of the field. The three planes, machine guns stuttering, swept in together on the slow-moving ship.

Watching them bullet-dive toward him, Wentworth saw certain death for his valiant men and himself. Their ship made a perfect target. He snatched out his automatics and sprayed lead at the lights that flooded the field with pale lavender illumination. His bullets smashed them into blackness and he sent his shout against the beat of the propeller, the lowered hum of the motor.

"Ground loop!"

He felt the ship tilt to the left as Ram Singh threw over the stick. There was a rending crash, the snarl of a bent propeller and Wentworth was hanging in his straps from an overturned plane. He was the first out and Jackson and Ram Singh were scarcely a second behind. They were jarred, but unhurt, and they followed Wentworth in a dash for the darkened hangar a hundred feet away.

Over their heads, motors roared and machine guns chattered. There was a beating of hard, leaden rain upon the earth near them, but none came too close and they reached the hangar in a hard run.

Inside the hangar, the liquid pop of a blow gun was incredibly loud. Wentworth cursed at this new attack. His gun answered almost of its own volition. There was a gasped cry and, after that, silence.

"Ram Singh!" Wentworth ordered sharply, "There must be a car outside. Get in it and speed away from here."

"Where to, *sahib?*"

"Philadelphia. Shake off pursuers there, not before. Report to *missie sahib.*"

There was a movement of shadows, a muttered: *"Han, sahib!"* and Ram Singh had salaamed and vanished. Within a minute and a half, an automobile engine roared and dwindled rapidly into the distance. Wentworth and Jackson stood with their backs against the left wall of the hangar and waited.

"Any orders, major?" Jackson asked quietly.

"Just wait," Wentworth told him "It's their first move. Must be more men here than the one Jivaro with the blow gun. Some will follow Ram Singh, thinking we've all escaped. When the others leave, we follow. The headquarters must be somewhere near here." Wentworth was hard put to hide the elation in his voice. He had played in luck tonight in spite of the destruction of his Northrup and his failure to capture a man alive in the battle under the wharf.

The machine guns had ceased to fire now and from the drum of the motors, it was apparent the planes were circling the field. Minutes dragged past, then a single flood light sprayed its ray over the ground. A second and a third followed and without waiting for complete illumination, the three ships swooped to a landing, rolled toward the hangar. From behind the lights, a dozen Indians in short scarlet kirtles ran toward the planes.

Goggled men sprang from the cockpits and the Indians prostrated themselves upon the ground. Wentworth watched, frowning, from the shadows of the hangar where, with Jackson, he crouched behind a gasoline drum. He was frowning, but what was going out there was obvious enough. The Indians believed these flying men were gods… One of the Jivaros leaped to his feet and raced off across the field. Moments later, all was dark again, but the planes were not trundled toward the hangar. There was absolute silence….

"Something's up, sir," Jackson whispered.

WENTWORTH'S EYES were tight and hard as he strove to accustom them to the darkness. No doubt that what Jackson said was correct. In some way, the Indians had detected his trick of sending only Ram Singh away as a decoy.

"Looks like we'll have to fight our way out," he said quietly. "Try to capture a white man. The Indians wouldn't know anything and wouldn't talk if they did. There must be a side door…."

Leading the way, with Jackson just behind him, Wentworth

They were dragged before the
throne of the Bat Man!

crossed the dark hangar toward its opposite side. He found the

door all right, turned the knob cautiously. That silence outside was prolonging itself suspiciously....

A voice called hollowly from the main door and Wentworth wheeled that way, guns ready. No one was in sight.

"Surrender!" the voice called again, "or you will be killed instantly."

Wentworth pushed open the side door and slipped outside. Jackson was close behind him and they stood, waiting, peering into the darkness that crowded close upon them. A dozen yards away was a thick woods. Nothing moved… With the abruptness of a gunshot, light bathed the entire side of the hangar, outlined the two men against it like black silhouette targets. Wentworth's gun blasted even as he flung himself to the earth. The light went out but behind him Jackson cursed raspingly.

"Got me, major. Blowgun dart…" His voice faded and was punctured by a series of popping sounds there in the edge of the woods. Wentworth's guns blasted, his lips thinning back from his teeth. Jackson, good God, Jackson hit by a poisoned dart!… Two darts pricked his own skin, one on the throat, the other on his cheek. A dozen more thudded gently against the galvanized side of the hangar. With a shouted roar of anger, Wentworth leaped to his feet.

God! So the Spider had got it at last, dying not by the guns of the Underworld, but by poison on the end of a primitive arrow! His automatics blasted deafeningly. Screams beat upon his ears through the thunder of his weapons, but it was the end. No mistaking that this time. Here was no death trap; no plant he could wriggle out of, here was only death….

Already a cold numbness was stealing over him. He wavered on his feet, squeezing the triggers of his automatics again. They kicked from his hands. For long seconds more he stood there, feeling again and again the prick of the darts, piercing his clothing, kissing his hands. By sheer will force, he fought down the numbness that washed up his limbs, that groped with cold fingers for his heart, his brain....

A fierce, ringing cry welled up from his lips. The Spider fell... A single glimmer of consciousness remained. He felt a great peace, a welling happiness of spirit. The battle was ended at last. Nita, *Nita*....

He was dead, and yet he continued to realize dimly what was going on about him. In this fumbling way, he felt that he was lifted and carried. He remembered vaguely that *curare*, the poison with which the South American blowpipe users tipped their darts, paralyzed instantly, but did not kill for almost twenty minutes. He was passing through that intermediate stage of death now....

Something pricked his throat. What the devil, were they injecting more poison into his veins? But there was no need for that. He was already... But was he? The numbness was receding, the blackness withdrawing from his eyes. He could not understand all that was happening, but he could not doubt it. Had these Indians then found an antidote for the poison that had no antidote?

HE HEARD a voice as harsh and grating as the squeak of a bat ranting impatiently. Then someone systematically began to slap his face. He opened his eyes and peered up into the impassive face of an Indian. The eyes glittered like points of obsidian knives... Hands gripped his shoulders and hauled him to his feet. He was in an immense black room where the light was dim and red. The grating voice came from a great bat upon a throne of skulls… what, a bat? But it wasn't possible…!

Wentworth shook his head violently to clear it, peered again at the throne. He saw now that it was a man seated there, a man with great leathery wings stretching from his shoulders. Now and then he waved them back and forth languidly. Wentworth saw these things without actually taking them in, but presently the last of the fogginess lifted from his brain, leaving it brilliantly clear. He peered into the face of the creature on the throne and, uncontrollably, a strong shudder plucked at his muscles. Was this the Bat Man then?

The face was incredibly hideous, the nose sliced off, the whole countenance drawn up toward that wound into a striking and hideous semblance of a bat's convoluted face. He had even attached huge, pointed ears to his head, and those wings… Wentworth pulled himself together with a bracing of his shoulders, a lift of his chin. There was that about the man and his face that made his blood run cold, but it was trickery. It must be….

He looked about him with steady eyes, saw that Jackson stood nearby with four men clinging to his unbound arms even as Wentworth realized he also stood. About them stood ranks of impassive Indians, each kirtled in brilliant red with a belt about their waists of some curious whitish leather…. The monstrous squeaking of the Bat Man pulled his head toward the throne sharply.

"You are wondering why you are alive," he rasped. "It is not our habit to kill such prisoners as come our way that is, not at once. You were shot with narcotic instead of poisoned darts. You see, our bats must have food."

He said the words simply, so matter-of-factly that for a moment the meaning did not penetrate. Food for the bats… But these bats were vampires. They fed on blood! Wentworth's eyes tightened against a tendency to widen. He could feel the quivering of the muscles in his temples, but Wentworth forced his stiff lips to smile.

"I have considered many ends," he admitted casually, "but supplying oral transfusions to bats was not among them!"

He was conscious of Jacobson's white face, his knotted, wide-muscled jaws, but he dared not look that way lest his sternly held composure desert him. The Bat Man made no direct reply to Wentworth's jibe, but the already contorted face was made revoltingly hideous by a frown. Jackson's breath was audible to Wentworth, a hissing, strangled sound. Somewhere behind the throne, a gong lifted its singing note and the Bat Man's frown faded. He smiled and lifted his right hand….

Behind the throne, a door opened, revealing hangings of golden silk and through those portieres stepped a woman with glistening black hair that fluffed out from beneath scarlet fillets. She wore a scarlet robe, but one milk-white shoulder was bare, her breasts were outlined in bands that criss-crossed over her bosom in Roman style. Wentworth's teeth locked tightly.

"June Calvert!" he whispered.

The girl smiled down on him haughtily, her dark intelligent eyes half-veiled by their lids.

"Who is this!" she asked imperiously.

THE BAT MAN'S rasping voice seemed to soften a little. "Richard Wentworth, my dear, who is either a confederate of the Spider, or the Spider himself!"

Wentworth controlled the start that his muscles involuntarily made at those words. What, had he been discovered so early in the fight? His fists knotted and the Indians to each side, feeling his muscles harden, gripped more tightly, put their weight into their holds upon his arms.

"One of my men," the Bat Man was explaining, "saw the Spider knock bats into a car driven by a Hindu and later the Hindu released those bats coated with radioactive paint. This man attempted to trail them from the skies. The Hindu is this man's servant...."

A remarkable change had come over June Calvert's face. It was still imperious, but it was twisted with hatred and rage. Her eyes, half-veiled, burned with living fires of anger and her hands became claws.

"The Spider she whispered. "The Spider who killed my brother!" Her hand slipped to her girdle and whipped out a curved dagger. She moved toward Wentworth on slow, crouching legs like a cat.

Wentworth smiled at her. "I am not the Spider," he said quietly, "but if I were, I would not have killed your brother. He died by the bite of bats."

June Calvert laughed and the sound was more like a snarl. "Yes, bats killed him. His own bats. He was a partner of the Bat Man, but you turned the bats upon him. It was you, you, *you...!*"

"Calm yourself, my dear," Wentworth shrugged. "I'll admit that anger becomes you...."

June Calvert sprang toward him with her knife uplifted. The Bat Man squeaked. It was precisely that—not words, nor articulate sound—simply a squeak of peculiar timber. An Indian sprang between Wentworth and June, offered his breast to the knife. For a moment, it seemed she would strike him down to reach the man behind him, but the Bat Man was speaking now.

"My dear," he whispered raspingly, "I have another, juster, more delightful death in store for our friend here, be he Spider or not. As you know, the appetite for human blood of our cutely starved bats must be whetted. Sometimes when we have no prisoners, we are forced to call for volunteers from among our company, but now there is no need for that. Would you not consent, my dear, to feed him to the bats instead?"

June Calvert stood panting, just beyond the human barrier which shielded Wentworth. Gradually the hatred and rage in her face became more subtle, gave place to a cruel joy.

"Splendid!" she whispered. "Oh, splendid!" She turned toward the throne and bowed low. "Grant that I may watch the... bats feed."

The Bat Man's laughter was squeaky, too. It ascended the scale like the grating of a saw-file until it became inaudible in the ultra-human range.

"Yes, my dear," he whispered. "You may!"

He lifted his left hand in a peculiar gesture and Wentworth's captors wrenched him backward and pinned him to the floor. Other Indians tore his clothing from his body. To his right, he could hear Jackson cursing and fighting futilely against similar treatment. Then, birth-naked, they were thrust across the darkened room. Behind them, came a long file of Indians, marching, chanting a harsh paean. Their joy was obvious. On the throne at the other end of the long room, the Bat Man laughed and laughed his squeaky, unearthly mirth and June Calvert stood, proud in scarlet, with a cruel smile on her lips.

WENTWORTH AND Jackson marched side by side now. Jackson twisted about his head. "Good God, what a woman!" he whispered. "She's mine, Major. Mine! I never saw a woman who could stir me so...."

Wentworth looked curiously as this staid soldier who had fought beside him through so many life and death struggles. A steady man, reliable and unimaginative. But now his chest heaved with something more than his exertions, and there was a set, determined jaw. He did not even seem to consider what lay in store for them.

"When we get out of this," Jackson said heavily. "I'm coming after her. I am."

Wentworth smiled thinly. Jackson said *when*, not *if*, we get out of this. But then, Jackson was depending on the Spider, who had wrested him from many a fierce and loathsome doom. Wentworth felt the grimness of his own locked jaw, but he was fighting against an overwhelming despair. To be locked in a cage, naked, with starved vampire bats, could mean only inevitable death.

A steel grating was opened in a chamber whose walls were steel-mesh wire. Wentworth was hurled forward, Jackson behind him. They sprang to their feet as the door clanged shut, got their backs against a wall and strained their eyes into the twilight of their death-chamber. There on the floor were stretched two things that had been men. Their flesh was shrunken and folded in upon their bodies. Cheeks were sunken and shriveled lips bared locked teeth. But more than anything else, it was the *pallor* of the bodies that mocked Wentworth and Jackson in the cage of bats. Those bodies were… bloodless….

Jackson still seemed in the daze which the beauty of the woman had afflicted upon him. Wentworth slapped him violently on the cheek.

"Later, Jackson, later," he said sharply. "Now, we must fight for our lives, unless you want to be as they are." His rigid pointing arm, indicating the bodies on the floor, snapped Jackson to attention. He paled. A shudder convulsed his shoulders.

"Good God, major!" he whispered. "What can we do?"

Wentworth shook his head slowly. There were Indian guards outside the cage with ready blowguns. There was no escape there. June Calvert had had a chair brought to the door and she sat there, languidly waiting for the torture to begin.

"What in God's name can we do?" Jackson whispered again.

Already above them in the dark upper reaches of the mesh prison, there were premonitory squeakings and fluttering. A bat winged through the air near them, circled, and swept toward Jackson. He struck savagely with his fist, then cursed and gripped his hand.

"The devil nipped me," he growled. Wentworth laughed and there was a touch of wildness in the sound. The bats' teeth were not poisoned, it was apparent, since Jackson had been bitten and still lived. But how long could they survive the blood-draining battle with the bats? There were thousands of them up above, to judge from the sound. But he knew the answer. It would be a matter of time only.

"We could make a barricade of those two bodies," Jackson said, without hope.

They did that, crouched behind the blood-drained corpses that warned them of what the future held. They settled themselves to fight for their lives. Abruptly the air was filled with a myriad black flutterings. Jackson and Wentworth flailed the air with their arms. Utter loathing gripped the Spider. The stench of the bats was nauseous and the thought of dying to feed such beasts....

Jackson screamed with a hint of hysteria. "Take him off! Take him off!"

Wentworth smashed a bat that had fixed on the side of Jackson's face, then he felt leathery wings touch his throat and tore a vampire from his own flesh. Black wings were beating in his eyes. His breath came short and hot in his throat and it strangled him. He fought with locked teeth, without hope, but with desperation. Good God above, what an end for a man...!

CHAPTER 9
THE WOOING OF NITA

NITA WAS reluctant to leave the Early Quaker with Fred Stoking and his party, knowing, as she did, the battle that impended. But there was nothing she could do to help Wentworth when the bats came, so she went at his bidding. The evening dragged at the night club to which they went and at midnight the group broke up. Newspaper boys were shouting extras when Fred Stoking helped Nita into a taxicab. The headlines screamed of the massacre at the Quaker.

Stoking looked at Nita, sitting erect though pale in the dim rear of the cab, then leaned toward the driver and ordered him to make all possible speed to the Quaker hotel. Nita thanked him with a glance. There could be no news of Dick there, unless… unless, she forced the thought, he had fallen prey to his enemies. But she must know that much with all speed. She was scarcely conscious of the blond handsome man beside her, whose eyes were so attentively on her face. Her thoughts were all of Dick….

The Quaker was a shambles and police sought to bar Nita and her escort, but Stoking was equal to that emergency. He and his family were influential; Commissioner Harrington was a personal friend… They went in, but found no news of Wentworth. Nita brightened a little. He had found a trail then, and followed it.

Stoking led Nita into a small lounge off the main lobby and seated her there.

"I'm sure you won't go to sleep for hours," he said.

Nita acknowledged that with a faint smile. Did she ever sleep when the Spider was abroad? Well Wentworth knew that and he would phone her when there was opportunity… She sent word to the desk where she might be found… Stoking found his way to the deserted bar and brought back drinks he had mixed himself.

"Now, Nitita," he said, "let's talk."

There was something in his tone that pulled Nita's head toward him, that penetrated her consciousness. She often worried about her Dick, but it seemed tonight that her fears were greater than usual. It was almost as if she sensed that at this very moment, far away in New Jersey, Wentworth was being thrust into the cage of famished vampires. But she could not know that of course. She forced herself to attend to Stoking's words….

"Nitita," Stoking said again, using the name that he had given her long ago in pig-tail-pulling days. "Nitita, you are unhappy." He rushed on as she tried to protest. "It is not a secret, you know. When I came back from the Orient, you were the first person I asked for, and I heard such tales! Nitita, you have no right to be unhappy."

Nita laughed a little unsteadily. She looked up into the handsome face bending protectively toward her. Fred Stoking had always had nice eyes. They had acquired authority and depth with the added years, and they were tender on hers now.

Nita said, hesitantly, "Why, Fred, I believe you're making love to me!" She knew instantly that it was the wrong thing to have said. Stoking leaned closer.

"Nitita, you'll say I'm a romantic fool, but I always have loved you. Ever since…."

Nita lifted her hands in mock horror. "Not that line, Fred, please. The fiction writers have abused it so!"

Stoking refused to banter. He reached up and touched Nita's gleaming hair with a caressing finger. "I'm very serious about this, Nitita."

NITA WAS silenced. There was an intent directness about this man that could not be turned away with jests. She looked into the depths of his eyes and believed him. Her hand went impulsively to his.

"Don't, Fred," she said quietly. "I appreciate what you say, more than you can know. But I'm engaged to another man."

Stoking threw back his head and laughed. There was an edgy bitterness to the sound that was not pretty. "Engaged!" he said mockingly. "For how many years, Nita, have you been engaged to Dick Wentworth?"

Nita took her hand away and twisted her slim white fingers together in her lap. She looked at them, writhing there, and she smiled. "It's quite a while," she said quietly.

"He has no right!" Stoking declared fiercely. "I stayed away because I know of this so-called engagement, but as it went on and on, I began to hope. Nita, I came home for you. I am going to take you back with me. No man has a right to inflict such unhappiness on any woman...."

Nita lifted her head proudly. Her hands were quiet now. There might have been a time when domineering thrilled her, but she was a woman who had... good God, who had killed men! These slim white hands of hers could throw a bullet with accuracy that almost rivaled the Spider's. Her muscles were hardened by the physical instruction Wentworth had insisted she undertake when, defying his own opposition and the dictates of her own longings for normal, human life; she had pledged herself to the hard road of the Spider. Why, if she wished, she could tie even this powerful man beside her into knots with *jiu-jitsu!* No, she could not be cave-manned.

Stoking saw his error at once. "Forgive me, dear, if I sound too excessively masculine," he said, with a touch of whimsicality, "but you can't guess how long I've eaten out my heart with longing."

"Stop, Fred," she said softly, "you make me very unhappy!"

Stoking laughed again, harshly. "Then I will stop. You have enough unhappiness… Oh, my dear, I could give you so much. I know you do not love me, but you would, Nitita, you would! Don't tell me that you don't like the things I do, the far ends of the earth when you wish, and a fireside and children when you don't. Unhappiness!"

Nita's full lips straightened themselves with compression. "You are talking rather foolishly," she said, for all the stab of pain he had given her. Fred Stoking could read her all right. "Very foolishly. After all, I am, as the saying goes, free, reasonably white, and considerably over twenty-one…."

"Twenty-six," Stoking said harshly. "Can you tell me anything about you I don't already know?"

"A great deal," Nita smiled into his eyes, so directly, so steadily that his own faltered a little. "A very great deal, Fred. But what I am saying is this: I am not unhappy in my present life. If there are… other things I would like, you must not think that I took my present course without great thought. It may be that Dick and I shall never marry. Dick warned me of that when we found we loved each other. He was unwilling for me to face that, but

I insisted. We… love each other. I don't know what more to say." She reached for his hand, confidently now, steadily and he gripped it hard with both of his. "Fred, I've told you a great deal more than any one else has ever heard. I tell you so you won't foolishly nurture a vain hope… If after all you're not merely… but that was unkind. I believe you and what you say."

STOKING HELD to her hand fiercely, his face drawn and lined with his struggle for control. His voice came out hoarsely. "All right. I accept what you say. But that doesn't mean I give up. Not if Wentworth said the things you indicate. And he would. I know it now. He would be the first to give me encouragement!"

Nita gasped, her hand flinching from his grasp. Before her rose the face of the man she loved, not the gay smiling Dick who first had won her love, but the white-faced battler whom peril created. She saw the hard bitterness that wrenched his lips, the cold, gray-blue strength of his eyes, and she could hear him saying just what Stoking declared.

"Darling, you know it is hopeless," he would say. "I love you. God knows I do. Love you enough to give you up. Seek happiness in normal living. The hell in which the Spider lives is not for a glorious woman like you…."

Nita buried her face in her clenching hands. "No!" she cried, her voice muffled, "No, no, no!"

Stoking sat silent beside her, a little frightened at the emotion he had stirred, but his lips were grim-set. He was a fighter, too. Presently he touched Nita's arm.

"We'll forget it for the present," he said, "but don't think I've finished. I don't give up so easily."

There was a bleak coldness in his own blue eyes. He looked up abruptly as a movement caught his gaze. A bellboy stuck his head in at the door. "Phone call for Miss Nita van Sloan!"

Nita sprang to her feet. "Where?" The boy turned and swaggered cockily across the lobby. Death nor tragedy, nor weeping women in the hotel lounge, could dim the brass that shone upon him—and not alone from his uniform buttons. Nita hurried to the telephone he indicated, aware that Stoking followed at a discreet distance. Now, Nita thought, now I'll hear Dick's voice. Dear Dick…!

"Hello," she faltered, then she straightened, her hands tight on the telephone. The happiness went out of her, but something else entered, the white, tight-lipped determination that was the other woman beneath her soft and lovely beauty. She spoke in Hindustani, her voice crisp, decisive.

"Is he in his own identity, Ram Singh, or…? That helps some. Where are you? Wait there then. I'll come as quickly as possible. No, Ram Singh, there is nothing you can do now but wait."

She turned from the phone and Stoking strode toward her. He checked a half-dozen feet away, recognizing the change in her. It was present even in the way she walked. Still graceful she was, but there was business and determination in her pace.

"It's trouble," Stoking said flatly. "I've heard how you've gone to rescue Wentworth on occasion. You'll have to count me in on this."

Nita hesitated and her appraisal of him was as swift and competent as a marine captain's. "Very well," she said. "Get the fastest car and the fastest plane in the city. Have the car at the door in five minutes; the ship ready when we reach Camden field. Dick has been captured by the Bat Man!"

She moved swiftly to the elevators and for a space of seconds, Stoking stood and watched her go, his eyes admiring, filled with longing, then he sprang to a telephone....

IT WAS just four minutes later that Nita stepped from the elevator, but Stoking was ready. He caught her elbow and was conscious of the bulge of a gun beneath the smart, tailored fit of her dark blue suit. Stoking felt distinctly out of place in his tail coat and faultless evening dress, but he made a joke of it.

"I carry armament, too," he told her gaily, "part of which you would probably disapprove. It is a knife strapped to my left forearm."

Nita said briefly, "Knives have their uses. Ram Singh has saved my life a dozen times over with his. Is the rest of your armament a revolver? If you have no firearms, I have an extra one in my purse for you."

They were in the car by now—Stoking's own, with a respectful chauffeur at the wheel—and the machine, which was a rakish Minerva, was muttering at close to top speed through the deserted streets. Stoking lounged on the cushions beside Nita and she noted with approval that he had the same manner of facing crises that so distinguished Wentworth, a calm, bitter readiness. Nita herself was tense.

"Don't you want to tell me about it?" he suggested quietly.

"You'll have to know if you're to help," Nita conceded, as if reluctantly. She told him of Wentworth's flight, the crash, and of Ram Singh's being sent away in a stolen car. "Ram Singh knew that he was supposed to be a decoy," she went on, "and when the Bat Man's crew didn't pursue, he stopped. He heard some fast, deliberate shooting and recognized Dick's guns. Then he heard Dick cry out…" Nita paused, pressing her hands tightly down on the bulging black handbag in her lap. "Ram Singh does not scare easily, but he said that it… it sounded like a devil's death cry."

"Dick isn't dead:' Stoking said quietly. "You would have known it, if he were."

Nita's voice was very low. "Yes, you do know me, Fred. You're right, I would have known. What Ram Singh said confirms it. He saw Dick and Jackson carried into two planes and flown away. Ram Singh tried to steal the third plane, but found the propeller had been bent in landing. He just escaped the Indians and came to phone me. He's in Flemington. We're flying there. Have to make a landing in a field with magnesium flares."

"I've got a two-seater Lockhead Vega," Stoking said casually. "I'm an indifferent pilot, but I understand you can handle ships."

"I have a thousand hours—transport license," Nita replied, tight-lipped. That was Dick's doing, too, teaching her to fly. Dick had been thorough….

"I want to apologize again," Stoking kept his tone light, "for trying to caveman you. It was not the right tactic—not at all!"

Nita felt her tension easing a little beneath his banter. He was doing his part well, but even he knew that the ultimate effort must be hers. Well, she had never failed Dick yet.

The Vega was fast as Nita could have wished, but it seemed scarcely to move toward Flemington. She made a safe, though rough, landing on a meadow near the town and Ram Singh raced up in a car while they still clambered from the plane. The Hindu hesitated at sight of Stoking but, at a sign from Nita, accepted him and began to spill what supplementary news he had in a virtual downpour of words.

"What were the Bat Man's planes used for?" Nita asked abruptly.

Ram Singh lifted his shoulders in token of ignorance. "Perhaps, *missie sahib*, to distribute bats. There was a cage of them in the plane left behind."

Nita laughed exultingly. "To the field quickly, Ram Singh!" she cried as she sprang into the car Ram Singh had brought. "We must have that cage of bats!" The car was fast enough, but scarcely comfortable. Stoking and Nita jounced miserably as the intrepid Hindu streaked over dark Jersey roads. He battled curves with squealing tires and motor roaring wide open, flew through unlighted anonymous towns that were no more than sounding boards for the car's engine.

"Why this wild enthusiasm for bats?" Stoking inquired mildly. "I must confess the poisonous little beasts don't interest me in the least."

"Later," Nita snapped. "Look for barbed-wire fences. If you see one, sing out. Ram Singh, stop at the first cry. *Stop, Ram Singh!*" Nita sprang from the car, groped in a pocket of the front door and got pliers, then strode to a barbed-wire fence on her side of the road. Within brief minutes, she was back with a coil of separate strands of wire. But still Stoking had no time for questions. Nita demanded his handkerchief, then the lining from his coat. Finally, she tore the upholstery of the car with the pliers and pulled out gobs of curled hair and padded cotton.

Ram Singh was traveling more slowly and silently. Everything in his manner suggested that they were near the field and that no chances must be taken of discovery.

"Bring me the cage of bats," Nita ordered.

Ram Singh sprang from the car and salaamed profoundly, lifting cupped hands to his forehead as he bowed in respect. *Wah!* This woman was a fit mate for his master—a tigress whose claws were as deadly as those of the old one himself. Bring back the bats? He would bring back heaven and hell, let her but command it!

As he strode off into the darkness, Nita sprang from the ear and took the cap oil the gasoline tank. She had fastened the torn bits of cloth to strands of the barbed wire and now she dipped each one into the gasoline. When Ram Singh returned, she was ready. At her command, the Hindu maneuvered out one of the bats and held it so it could not bite. Nita fastened a string made of torn cloth through a small slit she made in the bat's inter-femoral membrane. The string was attached to wire, which in turn wrapped a bundle of gasoline-soaked cloth.

All climbed bade into the car, then Nita touched a match to the gasoline rag and ordered the bat released. With the torch blazing behind him, the bat rose bewilderedly straight upward for a short distance. Then, with side excursions in which it tried to shake off the blazing tail that had been given, it made a laborious way southward. Nita watched until the ball of fire gave her the right direction, then she sent Ram Singh forward.

The Hindu was smiling broadly. *Wah!* Had he not said she was a veritable goddess? Wentworth *sahib* had sprayed bats with luminous paint and followed them. The *missie sahib* lacked the paint, but did that hinder her? By Siva, no! They would follow these bats to the hiding place of this unclean creature who flew through the air, then, by Kali, the destroyer, there would be an accounting! A hand stole to the hilt of the keen knife at his sash....

They traveled five miles southward before Nita released the second bat. That left her three more. When they were gone.... But before that, they must have a clue to the Bat Man's whereabouts. They *must!* One by one those bats with their trail of fire fought upward into the sky and winged their way off into darkness, charting a course for the Bat Man's headquarters. The way was still southward. The next to the last bat had almost escaped them when the rays of an approaching car's headlights blinded them, but finally they detected the flying creatures deviating from a straight, southern course, heading slightly eastward. They were near now, very near. That much was obvious, but how would they find the place with only one more bat? They might arrive within a hundred yards of the place and then....

RESOLUTELY, NITA prepared a larger bundle for the torch, burdened the final bat until it could scarcely lift itself toward the sky. It would be forced to fly slowly; the longer burning of the torch would help. Nita signaled to a stop, alighted and stepped behind the car to dip the cloth in gasoline. As she struck a match to the torch, she breathed a little wordless prayer. If this hope failed them... The bat struggled upward. Nita watched it go with aching eyes, then whirled as footsteps grated in the roadway. Flashlight glare assaulted her eyes and a gruff voice that carried the obvious burden of authority, rasped at them to: "Put them up!"

"We've got you, you damned murderers!" another man rejoined. "You was seen turning loose them bats along the road. Guy passed you and saw you. And now we catch you at it."

One man was on the running board with a gun against Ram Singh's side. Nita did not answer. She barely heeded them or realized their presence now, for she was watching the ball of fire that marked the bat's heavy flight as it moved directly eastward....

"You're completely wrong about this," Stoking said sharply. "We have nothing to do with the poisoned bats. We...."

A policeman's stocky figure came out from behind the light and his billy slapped Stoking unconscious to the ground. "Any guy that would turn loose them bats..." he muttered, then turned to Nita.

Nita realized abruptly that, though she had at last approximately discovered the hiding place, at least of adherents of the Bat Man—the spot where possibly Dick was held prisoner—she was now helpless to render him any assistance. She caught the policeman by the arm, tried to explain what they had been doing. He only scowled and growled at her.

"Listen, baby," he said. "Only one thing int'rests me. You was turning loose them bats and you are going to jail. Come along!"

Nita gazed despairingly into his face. He couldn't mean what he said—but it was obvious that he did. She *must* get away. She had to save Dick—who must be very close now.

With a wrench, she freed herself from the policeman's hand and darted for the shrubbery at the side of the road. She reached it, but the bushes were thick and blocked her retreat. She snatched for the automatic beneath her arm, her breath sobbing in her throat. Dick never fired on police, not even to save his own life, but, but… this was for Dick!

She lifted the automatic. The policeman's stick slashed down on her wrist. Agony raced up her arm, then the policeman had her. Her arm was twisted behind her back until she moaned with the pain of it. She was tripped and thrown flat on her face, then handcuffs pinched home on her wrists. She lifted her head and saw Ram Singh unconscious on the ground beside Stoking. That hope was gone, too.

"Baby," growled the policeman, "when I say jail, I mean *jail!*"

Utter despair shook Nita. Sobs rose in her throat, but she choked them down. Surely, this time, destiny conspired against Dick! Was this then, the end which the Spider and his mate had known must come some day…?

CHAPTER 10
IN THE VAMPIRE'S CAGE

IT SEEMED to Wentworth, in the cage of the vampires, that he and Jackson had fought for hours against the bats. His arms became leaden with the ceaseless flailing against never-tiring wings. The upper half of his body was bleeding from half a hundred tiny wounds, but as yet, none of them was serious. Both men were panting through brassy throats.

"Can't… keep it up… much longer, Major!" Jackson gasped beside him. The ceaseless whipping of his arms lagged for an instant and five of the brown furry beasts broke through his guard and darted at his face and throat. Jackson shouted, seized one in his fist and beat at the others with it. The captured bat squeaked and squealed and other vampires drew off, fluttering just out of reach of the defending arms of the men.

"Make it keep on squealing," Wentworth ordered sharply.

Jackson did, and while the bat shrilled its fright, the others held back.

"It won't last long," Wentworth panted.

"No, and there's no way out… unless Ram Singh comes."

Wentworth shook his head. "Sent him to Philadelphia. We'll have to get out of this ourselves." It was as if he knew that at this minute, within five miles of the house, Nita and Ram Singh and Stoking were helpless in the hands of the police. He knew a sickening despair. If he could only think… Already the truce of fright was ending and the bats were fluttering to the attack again. Through their black cloud, Wentworth gazed toward where June Calvert still sat watching. She was leaning forward, her face cruelly smiling.

"Behold your love, Jackson!" he cried, "how she enjoys your torture!"

Jackson, flailing again with weary arms, peered toward her and, even in the midst of pain, Wentworth saw that she still drew him; that the strange attraction held. A glimmering of an idea began to shine in his brain.

"Jackson," he said quietly. "We're going to the door, back to back. You face the door...."

Jackson turned a bewildered face toward him. "We'll be more exposed, sir."

"Quite," Wentworth conceded. "I'll stand first. Set your shoulders to mine and we'll walk across to the door."

Jackson was used to obedience. He knew that if Wentworth spoke, it was in furtherance of some definite plan. He did not question the strategy. After all, he had been a soldier. As Wentworth stood, Jackson sprang to his feet, and set his back against Wentworth's, walked slowly toward the door while they both struck out with their arms and kicked off the bats that flew low to attack their legs. They reached the grilled opening and Jackson pressed against it.

"Now, what, major?" he asked. His voice was strained and difficult.

Wentworth struck down a bat that bit at his face, caught another in his hand and held it, loudly squealing, before him. For a while the others held off. Wentworth laughed.

"Behold, Jackson," he cried, "the woman you love!"

Jackson did not answer, but Wentworth could hear his heavy, strained breathing. The bats continued to circle and with regular, sweeps of his arms, he drove them back. He waited. It was a faint hope that he entertained. Jackson's instantaneous, passionate interest in the woman was a strange thing, but its reason was clear. The woman herself was intense, strongly emotional.

117

NITA JAN SLOAN

The sight of her fancied enemy undergoing the torture of the bats made her breasts heave quickly. If she saw Jackson's overwhelming fascination, was it not barely possible that she might respond?

JACKSON WAS a vigorous, handsome man, with a rugged, wide-jawed, wide-browed face. His chest was banded with muscle and the glistening perspiration caught every highlight, emphasized every ligament contour. There was something primitive about both of them: this savage fighter who had been an incorrigible in the army until he fell under Wentworth's firm hand, and this woman who could delight in torture and death. Elemental, both of them.

The Spider could not turn to watch the woman's face or actions. The bats would not permit, and even a glimpse of his own watching eyes might disrupt the spell he sought to weave. He could feel the quicker pumping of Jackson's sides, and finally, because he strained his ears through the ceaseless squeaking of the bats, he caught June Calvert's, whispered words.

"Why... do you look at me... like that?"

Jackson made no answer. If he had guessed at Wentworth's plan, he gave no sign of it. Wentworth supposed that he was too much preoccupied with emotion to think at all.

The woman spoke again, more strongly. "Why do you look at me like that?"

Jackson boomed out his deep laughter. "Because I hate you!" he cried.

Wentworth's eyes tightened and he nodded slowly. A bat broke through his guard and fastened on his throat. He tore it loose and felt his flesh rip, too. He laughed softly, battled on. The woman's voice was closer now.

"You don't hate me," she said. "You don't! I can see it in your eyes!"

Jackson said nothing and when the woman spoke again, Wentworth started, she was so near!

"Why do you look at me like that?" she whispered.

No sound from Jackson, no more from the woman. Wentworth could hear the breathing of both. He seized a bat and made it squeal in pain. The sound was piercing, hurt the eardrums, but it no longer drove back the vampires. They lanced in over Wentworth's arms. One got past him and fastened on the side of Jackson's throat, but Jackson did not move to knock it off.

"The bat!" the woman whispered. "There's a bat on your throat. Take it off; please take it off!"

Jackson laughed again. "There will only be another. Let him stay and take his three ounces of blood."

"Please take it off," June Calvert cried. "Oh, there is blood on you, all over you."

Deliberately, Wentworth allowed another bat to slip past him and fasten on Jackson's upper arm.

Jackson spoke to the woman. "Come in here."

"No, *no!*" The woman was panting.

Jackson laughed, triumph in its sound. "You must."

After that, long silence, then Jackson's laughter again, the muscles tightening across his back. Presently, the woman sighed.

"You're hurting me," she whispered. "The bars. Wait, I will open the door."

Her footsteps hurried away. Jackson's weight sagged against Wentworth's back. "She's a devil," he whispered. "She takes my strength away. God, she's wonderful, wonderful...."

Wentworth said nothing, his mouth tightening as he continued the battle against the bats. Not much longer, thank God. A little more and they would be out of this cage of death. Even then, there would be fighting—but against humans, and a limited number of them—not against the winged vampires... He made a mental note that Jackson, after this, would be useless to him against the Bat Man.

The woman's footsteps were running when she returned. "I had to kill the man," she sobbed. "I had to. He wouldn't give me the keys."

METAL RASPED and Jackson sprang through the door. Wentworth whirled and went after him, slammed the cage shut. Jackson thought nothing of his escape. There was still one bat fastened to his arm, but it was the woman, leaning back in Jackson's embrace, who removed that. She pinched the vampire's throat and held it for a while, then dropped it to the floor. There was a smile on her red lips as she looked up into Jackson's face. She would have to go with them, Wentworth thought, or the Bat Man would put her in their place in the vampire's cage. He cast swiftly about the black-walled room for a means of escape.

His clothing still lay upon the floor and he donned such

pieces of it as were not impossibly torn. The bites of the bats were beginning to pain now. He was wrapped in their torture. He went back to Jackson and June Calvert.

"June, if you want him to live," he said sharply, "We'll have to get you both out of here quickly."

June Calvert looked at Wentworth without comprehension for fully thirty seconds, then she pulled herself out of Jackson's arms.

"Good God," she stammered, "what have I done? I have freed my brother's murderer!"

"I am not his murderer," Wentworth told her quietly. "I have nothing to do with his death, but you have freed us. If the Bat Man catches you, it will mean your death as well as ours."

June seemed still in a half-daze. She looked from Wentworth to Jackson and her gaze lingered longest there. Her face softened.

"Yon are right," she whispered, "We must escape. Come, I'll lead the way."

Wentworth motioned Jackson toward the remnants of his clothing upon the floor and, with a bound, he reached them and pulled them on. Wentworth had no weapon, nor did Jackson and June had only her curiously curved dagger.

"Are there any weapons we can get?" Wentworth asked.

June shook her head slowly. "The Bat Man allows none," she said. "None save his own and the blowguns of the Indians."

Wentworth thought grimly that the Bat Man did not trust his allies overmuch and nodded at the idea. That would be a help, perhaps.

"We would better leave at once," he said. "Soon the Bat Man will come back to see if we are dead, and then…."

June Calvert nodded. She led the way with the stealth of a cat toward a curtained wall, pulled it aside and revealed a narrow passageway. "At the end of this are three doors," she whispered. "The one to the right leads outdoors. After that, there is no way to escape save by fighting through."

She walked ahead, carelessly, with assurance and behind her Jackson and Wentworth made no sound. Wentworth had no intention of leaving, but he must have a weapon before he could carry out his plan to kill the Bat Man. Jackson and the girl must go….

There was no warning at all, but suddenly the hall ahead of them was crowded with the short, kirtled figures of Indians and a dozen blowguns were aimed at Wentworth and his companions. He whirled to retreat, but that way was blocked in the same way. There was no escape, not even by sacrificing his companions could the Spider win through to kill the Bat Man and rid humanity of this newest and most terrible scourge. For, to hold either girl or Jackson as a shield, would merely expose his back to the other force… Wentworth shrugged.

"We surrender," he said shortly.

From somewhere nearby, but out of sight, the Bat Man squeaked an order. "To the bat cage with them. Strip the woman and throw her in with them. She is a traitor. That was for your benefit, my friends, now I shall repeat the order in their own language…" The Bat Man broke into a gabbled tongue of the Indians. Instantly, they moved forward, half of them almost crawling to keep clear of the blowguns which the other half held ready.

Wentworth knotted his fists, his jaw set rigidly, but he knew it was useless. He would only bring on his own death, whereas if he submitted… But what hope lay that way? There would not again be an escape from the fangs of the vampires. He locked his teeth to hold back the curses of despair. Now, surely, there was an end of hope…!

IF WENTWORTH surrendered philosophically, June Calvert did not. She swept, raging, toward the line of Indians and they parted before her, and seized her from behind, swept her helpless to the floor with a garrote about her throat.

A hoarse shout tore from Jackson. He hurled himself toward the struggling girl. Her dagger was out and she slashed about with it, hamstrung an Indian so that he dropped, screaming, to one knee. She took a second man in the groin with the blade, Jackson seized an Indian about the throat with his powerful hands, lifted him high and tossed him upon his fellows. Then a tiny dart blossomed on his shoulder, the hollow pop of a blowgun echoed down the hall. From his place of concealment, the Bat Man laughed squeakily.

Wentworth had shouted a warning when Jackson first charged in, but he had known in advance that it was hopeless. Yet he could not stand back while these other two fought… The Spider's manner of fighting differed from theirs. Instead of rushing in against the blowguns, he threw back his head and laughed, an echo of the squeaky, bat-like mirth of the leader.

While be laughed, he walked toward the place where Jackson and June still battled.

The girl was almost unconscious now, with the bite of the garrote on her throat. Jackson was staggering and Wentworth thought from his behavior that the dart which had pierced his shoulder carried the narcotic, not the deadly poison... Wentworth continued his laughing advance. He could see that the Indians were puzzled, that they did not know whether or not to shoot. The Bat Man continued his mirth. Apparently, he could not see what went on in the narrow hallway. Wentworth stood now over Jackson, who had fallen, and the girl. Both were unconscious. Lord, it was so hopeless. What could he hope to accomplish, unarmed, against ten savages? Two lay dead on the floor, one still moaned over the gashed and useless leg....

Wentworth helped the injured Indian to his feet and, still making squeaking noises, led the man down the hall. The blowgun men were puzzled, and as he continued, parted their ranks. Hope began to thrill through Wentworth, but it died in an instant. Apparently, he had shown himself to the Bat Man, for suddenly a high, shrill squeak rang out. Instantly, a flood of Indians hurled themselves upon him. Blowguns were forgotten. It was hand to hand, twist and wrench and punch. An Indian seized Wentworth's right wrist and attempted to twist it behind him. The man was powerful and his very grip was painful. Wentworth hurled himself bodily backward, tossing the Indian against the ceiling with the impetus of his fall.

The trick was a mistake. Though the man he had thrown fell unconscious, and probably dead, to the floor, four other Indians dived bodily upon Wentworth before he could rise to his feet again. He held one off with a kicking foot, got his elbow against the throat of a second, but the other two hit solidly on his chest. One got his fingers on Wentworth's throat and pressed crushingly on the larynx. Darkness began to whirl before Wentworth's eyes. He pulled up his hands got hold of a finger with each and shredded the throttling hold off of his throat. He heard the fingers break and the Indian whimpered.

Another of the small, fierce men crawled into the battle. He had June's bloody knife and he moved its blade gloatingly toward Wentworth's throat. At the same time, five more Indians hurled themselves upon him, seizing arms and legs, kicking at his sides. Pain rippled over him. The knife caressed his neck… and a gun barked!

THE SOUND of the pistol was deafening in the narrow confines of the hall. The Indian with the knife jerked to his feet and crashed down again in a crumpled heap, his forehead smashed by a heavy bullet. Three pistol shots smashed out together and three more of the small, savage men were slain. Wentworth hurled a body from his chest, bowled over another Indian and sprang to his feet.

"Catch, Dick!" It was a woman's voice, and an automatic arched through the air to his hand. A woman's voice… Who could it be but Nita? Wentworth threw back his head and laughed joyously. Nita… and a gun in his hand again.

"Brave work, Nita," he cried. He charged down the hall where the Indians were scrambling for their blowguns. He fired once as a man got his long tube to his lips, then he ducked from the hallway into an opening to his right. He no longer heard the squeaking laughter, or sharp orders of the Bat Man, but the creature could not be far away. Back in the hall, Nita's gun and those other two he had not identified were slamming death into the Indians....

Wentworth was racing down a corridor between narrow walls, toward a twilight dimness that seemed to recede before him. He stopped abruptly, listening. The shooting and the shrieks of wounded and dying still came to his ears, but that was all. Nevertheless, be ran on, hoping against hope that he might find the Bat Man. Something clicked beneath his feet and he ducked backward, sensing an opening above his head. He went back three slow paces, eyeing that hole in the ceiling.

Suddenly he understood. A black form had dropped from the opening and leathery wings fluttered toward him. He cursed and fired a quick shot. No need to wonder whether the teeth of these bats were poisoned. Why else would a trap be set with them? He fired twice more in quick succession, then pulled his coat over his head, covered hands in pockets and raced past the spot where the bats whirled. He dared not use more of his bullets, lest there be none left when finally he came face to face with the Bat Man himself.

He burst suddenly into the open through a swinging door and stopped, peering about him. In the east, the sky was graying with dawn. In the woods that grew close to the house, sleepy birds were twittering with the promise of day. Wentworth looked down to the grass. It was wet with dew and here and there upon

127

the blades; spiders had woven webs which were beaded with moisture. Straight ahead of him, a spider web had been torn.

With a cry that be scarcely suppressed, Wentworth sprang forward. The trail in the dewy grass was plain now. This way, the Bat Man must have fled. Abruptly, as he ran, Wentworth halted, made a circuit beneath a tree. There, for some reason, the tracks had left a gap as if the Bat Man had sprung into the air for a distance of ten feet. Even so, Wentworth barely escaped the trap he more than half suspected. His feet jarred the hidden trigger and from the tree overhead a sprung branch hurled a spear deep into the earth where, moments before, Wentworth had narrowly missed treading. If he had stepped there, the spear would have drilled him from neck to groin. Thereafter, he went more cautiously along the woodland path. He had gone perhaps seventy-five yards when, ahead of him, a plane roared into life. Wentworth sprinted for the clearing which he could see now vaguely through the trees, but as he burst into the open, the ship he had heard was just lifting from the earth, despite a cold motor, and climbing rapidly over the tree tops....

THE AUTOMATIC jumped and slammed in Wentworth's hand. He was certain that he hit the plane twice before it slid out of range, but he could not have scored on the pilot for, though there was a slight faltering on the flight after the second shot, the plane kept steadily on. Wentworth cursed with disappointment. There could be no question that the Bat Man had escaped in that ship. He proceeded more cautiously along the trail back and found another trap which he had missed by sheer luck with his long, running stride. He discharged a small bow which hurled a poisoned dart.

Well, once more the Spider had met the Bat Man and this time, though he had failed to capture or kill the leader, he at least had not utterly failed. He was light-hearted as he loped back to the gaunt, low building where Nita had come to the rescue. The long, dim halls were as silent as before, more so, since cries and shots no longer echoed. For no apparent reason, an unrest seized him. His pace quickened until he fairly sprinted toward the place where they had battled.

Before he reached the spot, he saw bodies of red-clad Indians sprawled in the doorway. None of them even groaned. Surely, by now, he should hear the murmur of Nita's voice, the sound of her walking. But there was nothing… He hurdled the stacked bodies, halted motionless in the middle of the hallway. Save for the dead—and the unmoving body of June Calvert—the place was empty.

"Nita!" Wentworth sent the cry echoing. "Nita! Nita!"

He waited and the echoes died and silence flowed back to his waiting ears. He sprang toward the spot where she had stood, shooting down the foes that crowded against his back. On the floor there, he found a scrap of lacy white that was her handkerchief, found two abandoned automatics… He straightened with his face gone hard and white, his eyes glittering like deep glacial ice. There was no mistaking those signs, but, good God, Nita could not have been captured thus with those other two with her to help her fight! It wasn't possible…!

And then Wentworth saw another thing that filled his heart

with leaden despair. The wall was pricked in half a dozen places by blowgun darts. A groan came from the depths of his soul. He whirled and ran through other dim corridors, burst outside and circled the building, but nowhere was there any trace of Nita. Finally he came to a standstill again where her guns lay upon the floor. He lifted his clenched fists toward the ceiling and shook them twice. He had thought at least a partial victory was in his grasp, and in the moment of elation, he had lost everything…!

CHAPTER 11
AGAINST ALL HOPE

WENTWORTH TURNED once more to look about the hall and his eyes fell upon the supine body of June Calvert. Was she dead, then, with that garrote about her throat? With sudden hope, Wentworth approached her in long strides, looked down on her sullenly beautiful face. If it had turned blue with strangulation, then the stagnant blood already had been dissipated… He flung down on a knee and felt for the pulse, held his polished platinum cigarette case before her lips. There was no indication of life either way, and yet….

Swiftly, he turned June over on her face and began resuscitation, hands pressing down on her short ribs to expel air from her lungs, releasing sharply to suck in oxygen. Artificial respiration. He was desperately anxious that she survive. If she was seriously interested in Jackson, she might well reveal the Bat Man's secrets!

It was heart-breaking work, this resuscitation of an apparently lifeless woman. If she should survive, he might speed the rescue of Nita, the smashing of all the Bat Man's demon plans. But if his work was useless, precious minutes were being wasted. For over half an hour, he continued the slow rhythm of breathing. There was a frown upon his forehead and curious, straight hardness to his lips. Almost he had despaired when there was a faint sigh from June's lips and, sluggishly, reluctantly, her lungs took up their work again!

She was alive! Wentworth almost cried the words aloud. He had no stimulant to administer, but he used what means of restoration he had, bathing her temples with cold water from a tap he found. Fear widened her eyes when first she beheld him, but presently she appeared to remember the situation. She tried to look about her, hand gripping her throat....

"The Bat Man kidnapped them all," Wentworth told her harshly. "The woman I love, the man you love."

June Calvert thrust herself up on stiff arms and stared about the passageway; saw the heaped bodies of dead Indians and nothing more. Wentworth helped her to her feet and she began to stumble through the deserted halls and rooms. Finally, she sagged weakly against a wall and sobbed there, shoulders jerking spasmodically.

Wentworth watched her narrowly. He must judge her mood exactly if she was to be of help to him. Weeping was the wrong note. He jeered at her.

"I didn't expect you to spend time crying," he said. "Don't you realize that every second wasted brings the man you love that much nearer to the cage of vampires?"

June lifted her dark, disheveled head and stared into Wentworth's eyes. Her shoulders still jerked, but no sound came from her lips.

"Help me," Wentworth urged, "and we will save him."

Resolution hardened on the girl's face, a faint smile twisted her full lips. "You are not interested so much in saving him, as in capturing the Bat Man."

"Not capturing him," Wentworth corrected softly, *"killing him!"*

June Calvert's dark eyes widened a little, but she made no comment.

"But you are wrong about my not wanting to save Jackson." Wentworth continued. "He has been my comrade in arms for years. My Hindu servant is also a captive—and the woman I love. Come, June, the Bat Man Ordered your death. You can no longer have any loyalty toward him. And there is Jackson…."

"Jackson," she whispered. "A soldier? What's his first name?" **WENTWORTH FOUGHT** for calmness. Seconds were so precious, but if he took a wrong move with this girl… He smiled a little. "Jackson won't want you to call him by it," he said. "It's Ronald."

June was immediately indignant. "Why, I think it's a lovely name. Ronald," she tried it on her lips, softly. "Ronald Jackson."

Wentworth lost patience. "You'll never have a chance to call him by it if we don't hurry," he snapped. "Don't you realize that Jackson is going to be killed… by the Bat Man? Even while we stand here talking, he may be…."

June shuddered. The tremor shook her shoulders, jerked over

her entire body. "Yes, yes!" she whispered. "But I know so little. I don't know who the Bat Man is or where his other headquarters are, except that he boasted that only he could reach his hideout in the Rocky Mountains unless he went first and prepared the way...."

Wentworth was silent, letting her talk now that she was started, but bitter disappointment gripped him. Despair was a cold weight in his breast.

"... I think," June was frowning, "that he was... quite fond... of me. He had a strange diffidence and made me rather timid offers to sit beside him when he ruled the world. Oh, it's not as unlikely as you think. He intends to practically destroy the United States...."

A jagged curse forced itself from between Wentworth's lips. "But why? In God's name, why?"

"He intends to demand tribute of all the nations of the world," June said slowly, "in return for a promise not to loose the bats on their peoples."

"Preposterous!" Wentworth snapped. "They wouldn't pay." Then he frowned, remembering. There had been a time when nearly all the maritime nations of the world had paid tribute to the Barbary pirates of the Mediterranean, bribed them not to attack ships flying their flag. Only the United States had refused, and had sent great battleships to uphold that refusal. And that had been less than a hundred years ago. Only the United States had refused....

"He thought," June went on, "that the United States would refuse to pay, so he would make an example of her to the rest of the world. I think he plans to save New York for the last. His next attack...."

"You know that? Good!" Wentworth began to know hope again. "Where will that be?"

"Michigan City," June replied briefly.

Wentworth uttered a sharp exclamation. Michigan City was an amusement resort at Chicago to which the city's population flocked in teas of thousands for swimming and other amusements. And in the entire place, there were not a half-dozen buildings into which the bats could not enter. In Chicago proper, it would be different. But in Michigan City, literally thousands would die....

"Come," he said sharply, and hurried down the hall. He heard June's footsteps just behind him.

"Where are you going?" she demanded.

"Michigan City!"

"But you promised to save Ronald!" the girl cried.

Wentworth nodded, never slackening his pace as he pushed out into the morning that was reddening with sunrise. June Calvert caught his arm, tried to pull him about.

"You promised!" she cried. Wentworth stopped and faced her. "Do you know where Jackson is?" he demanded.

"No."

"Do you know where the Bat Man is?"

"N-No."

"Then, June, we have to go to the only place you know of that the Bat Man will appear, don't we?"

JUNE SOBBED, pressed a clenched hand to her forehead.

"Yes, yes" she whispered, "but before that, Ronald may be… may be…."

Wentworth's tanned face was drained of all color. June Calvert lifted her head slowly and looked at him. "Ah," she whispered, "I forgot. The woman you love is there, too!"

Wentworth said dully, "Yes," He turned and hurried off toward the airfield where, almost an hour ago, the Bat Man had winged into the dawn. June caught his arm.

"There are no more planes," she said. "There is nothing at all here to travel in, but there's a highway about three miles to the west."

They tramped in silence through the damp woodland, crashing over underbrush, jumping brooks, fighting thickets. Finally, they burst out in the highway and stopped, staring. There were two automobiles parked on the opposite side of the road. In one of them, two policemen sat.

Wentworth walked toward them and the man behind the wheel twisted about an angry face.

"Hey, buddy," he called. "Come here and get us loose, will you? We're all tied up."

Wentworth stopped beside the car. "How'd you get tied up?" he asked curiously.

"We was chasing them guys what's turning loose bats," the man, red-faced and angry, declared. "We has them all tied up, girl with them, too. Then one of them gets loose and pulls a knife on me and we can't do nothing."

Wentworth tackled the ropes, shooting eager questions at the policemen, but as the story unfolded, his eagerness died. It was apparent now that it was Nita the men had almost stopped. Nita and Ram Singh and Stoking. All of them were in the Bat Man's power now, food for bats. Wentworth's jaw tightened... The police took him and June back to town, casting many curious glances at the girl's strange scarlet dress. When they had found the dead Indians there in the woods, they would remember this meeting, because of that similarity of dress. Wentworth shook his head grimly. There was no time now to explain, even though trouble would follow later.

At Flemington, he found the plane Stoking had rented. He appropriated it and sent the ship racing into the West. At dusk, the attack would be made on Michigan City. There was ample time to reach Chicago by plane. Ample time, if there were no mishaps... Persistently, Wentworth's thoughts reverted to Nita. She was in this situation, prisoner of the Bat Man, because she had striven to help him. God, this was no life for a woman! Better a thousand times, if they had never met. Better if she Lad married this Fred Stoking, who had been her childhood sweetheart....

His bitterness came back overwhelmingly. What right did he have to wreck Nita's life this way, perhaps to bring about her death? If she had never met Dick Wentworth....

Wentworth was snapped from his reverie by a spluttering motor. He glanced sharply at his instruments, but nothing was wrong there and the engine was drumming steadily again. He peered over the side. Beneath him lay the wild reaches of the Alleghenies. Good God, if he were forced down here, it would take him days to reach even a mountaineer's cabin! Days more before he could reach Chicago! The Bat Man would have struck and vanished… The motor coughed and missed again!

THE SPIDER'S face became hard and rigid. No use to conjecture now. The engine was failing. It was only a question of selecting a spot to crash. A bitter curse squeezed out. He leaned over the side, staring down at the jagged, forested sides of mountains below him. He realized grimly that it was not merely a question of landing in a spot from which it might be possible to reach civilization, it was even doubtful if they would survive the landing!

There was not a fifty-foot clearing anywhere in the tangle of mountains—not a roadway, nor a fire lane. The motor was missing badly now. Even though he pulled the throttle wide, the plane was losing altitude. Not rapidly, but losing none the less. He would have to make his decision quickly.

A mountain-top glided by beneath him, its trees no more than seventy-five feet under the fuselage, and the valley beyond opened. Wentworth knew a thrill of hope, for there was clearly a break in the forest down there. He swept a rapid glance over the country. No sign of smoke, or of human habitation. He laughed sharply. Would it not be better to smash against that rocky precipice that thrust out of the opposite mountain? When finally he escaped from these mountains, Nita would be dead— and Ram Singh and Jackson… Every one dear to him would have died through his failure. Resolutely, he sought to close his mind to those facts. He was, he told himself, no longer a human being, but a cause. He was the Spider! He must live to defend humanity.…

Time after time, he had been compelled to abandon Nita to her fate while he battled new monsters of crime. For a single instant, however, his mind broke from his rigid control, and he pictured her thrown helpless into a cage of vampires, saw her white body fall under the fluttering black hordes....

He screamed curses into the air, shook his fist at the skies that arched pitilessly above. By God, it should not be! It should not be! The final splutter of the motor, the whir of the dying propeller snapped him out of his bitter tirade. He had been handling the plane sub-consciously, directing it toward that clearing in the valley which alone offered hope of safe landing.

Behind him, June Calvert's high voice beat on his sound-deafened ears.

"What's the matter?

"Motor conked out," he called back to her, then leaned over the side to stare down at the clearing. It was a lake, full of black, jagged snags. The trees grew right to its shores. Once more Wentworth laughed, hardly, bitterly. It would be better if he did die—but he must strive to live. He sent the ship down in a sharp dive....

CHAPTER 12
RACE WITH TIME

A S THE plane sloped toward the lake, Wentworth's eyes swept the wooded shores hopefully. There was no beach anywhere. The retractable landing gear already had been lowered. Now Wentworth set to work to crank it back into the fuselage by hand. The hull of the plane would not resist water long, but he could use it as a pontoon in landing whereas the wheels would catch and tip the ship forward on her nose. His danger, without the wheels, would be in snagging a wing in the water since they would be so close to the surface. Fortunately, the craft was a Lockhead Vega, a high-winged monoplane, so even that danger was reduced....

Swiftly the plane neared the mirror-like lake. The steep, wooded mountains were reflected and white clouds made their images below. It was strangely peaceful, but Wentworth knew no peace, only bitterness and mounting rage... Another hundred feet and the Vega would breast the lake. Wentworth kept the stick waggling gently from side to side, leveling off the wings. He swept in over the tree-tops with scarcely a dozen feet clear, put the nose down and swooped toward the surface.

Down the center of the lake, there was a space fairly clear of snags and Wentworth had picked that as the only possible landing place. Now, as the ship settled in a stall, only inches above the surface, he spotted a submerged log fairly in his path. There was no help for it. He must drive straight for the log. The stick had already gone soft in his hand... The ship squatted down on the water with a heavy impact, ran twenty feet and snagged the log....

"Let go and dive!" Wentworth shouted.

The nose went down, the tail whipped up and over, hurling Wentworth and June Calvert like catapult missiles through the air. Wentworth struck head first in a shallow dive, whipped to the surface and peered about for the girl. She broke water a few seconds afterward, smiled at him, white-faced.

"Don't worry about me," she gasped. "I can swim."

Side by side, they struck out for the shore. The plane, on its back, already was settling deep in the water, buoyed for a while by partiality emptied gasoline tanks. But the pull of the motor was rapidly overcoming that. Even as Wentworth reached the shore and stood erect in the edge of the woods, the water lapped over the last inch of canvas and the plane disappeared.

Wentworth, his face set, leaned forward to assist June Calvert to her feet and she looked despairingly into his face.

"We're beaten," she said dully. "Beaten before we fairly start!"

Wentworth's lips moved in a slight still smile, "It's ten o'clock. We have almost ten hours to reach Chicago."

June Calvert gazed into his strong face with its locked jaw and determined eyes and her own despair lessened. "But what can we do?" she whispered.

Wentworth turned and looked up the steep slope of the mountain, toward the bare outcropping of rock near its crest. He nodded toward it.

"From its top, we may be able to spot some help," he said. He turned toward the thick alder bushes that crowded close to the water's edge, the white-stemmed birches beyond. With a curt word, he started forward, wading first through swamp that rose to his knees. Among the birches, be stopped for a few minutes, whittling on two smaller trees with his pocket knife. Presently they went on again, each with a staff.

The thickets continued and briars snagged at his clothing,

tore his hands. He stopped and gave his coat to June Calvert. She thanked him with softening eyes, but his smile was thin.

"It's not chivalry, but wisdom," he said dryly. "You can travel faster with your shoulders protected."

SHE LAUGHED at him and they went on again, Wentworth crashing through ahead to break away. There was a hard desperation in his soul. He had to fight to keep from plunging forward at a mad run that would have exhausted him within minutes. A trotting horse travels farther, he reminded himself. God alone knew how much of this tramping there might be, but if he could get hold of a fast plane within the next six or eight hours....

After they left the low shores of the lake, the underbrush was thinner, but the grade was steepening. It took a half hour to reach the crest of the hill, Wentworth discovered with a despairing glance at his watch. Then twelve such hills... But there were the descents and the valleys to cross. Five, six such hills and his margin would be reduced to nothing.

"We'll have to run down this hill," he said shortly. "Jog, don't race."

He set the pace, the half-trot, half-lope that the woods-runners of the Indians had used over these same trails years ago. Halfway down the hill, they struck a small path and June cried out in happiness.

"See, a path!" she panted. "Some one must be near!"

"Game trail," Wentworth threw over his shoulder.

But he swung along its course. As long as it went in the direction he wished, it would be swifter traveling. Unconsciously, his

Wentworth was handling the powerful Boeing like a pursuit plane!

pace quickened. At the bottom of the hill, he realized that there were no footsteps behind him and halted. A hundred and fifty yards back, running doggedly at the pace he first had set, was June Calvert. Her red dress had been torn off at the knee and the coat looked strange with the silk robe, but she was plugging steadily along. She looked up, saw Wentworth.

"Go on, go on!" she cried. "I'm all right."

Wentworth waited until she was near, then ran on. The game trail stopped at a small brook in the valley, but another slanted up the hill, Wentworth pushed on, no longer running, but slowly regaining his breath as he pulled the hill. He had hoped from the ridge just passed, that he might detect some signs of human habitation. The hill ahead inspired him anew, but he said nothing… The next valley was empty of hope, too. Wentworth stole a glance at his watch, an hour and a quarter gone….

Doggedly, he held himself back as he loped down toward the valley. The game trail was gone now, wandering off down the valley and the way was constantly impeded by shrubbery. He kept his lips locked against the urge to pant. He could hear June Calvert gasp for breath. But, damn it, there could be no stop, no resting. Within a few hours, the Bat Man would strike. If the Spider did not then take his trail, it would be too late to save Nita and those two gallant men who had thrown in their lot with him. It might even be too late to strike at the Bat Man, for if this chance failed, future contacts would depend on luck alone.

These thoughts worked maddeningly in Wentworth's brain as he loped downhill, and labored up the next grade, the third. If this one also proved an empty hope… But it would only mean pushing on to the next and a further reduction of the possibility of success. He scarcely dared look at his watch.

It was hot in the woods where the trees choked off all breeze. Black flies and midges danced about his perspiring face and his shirt clung damply to his body. Nor were his shoes fitted to this type of walking. The soles speedily grew slippery on leaves and the fallen needles of pines so that walking became an exhausting labor. At the top of the third hill, June was three hundred yards behind him and he himself was panting through stubbornly resisting lips. Almost he dreaded to peer into the valley beyond and search the opposite slope, but hope urged him on. He looked—it was empty...!

JUNE CALVERT toiled up to him, glanced and passed on, pushing herself into a labored run. She was panting, too, but there was a stubborn set to her chin. Wentworth loped after her, drew abreast.

"What time?" she gasped. Wentworth looked reluctantly at his watch. "Half past twelve."

June said nothing and they ran on. At the bottom of the hill, a spring bubbled water into a small brook. Wentworth halted and they drank sparingly and pushed on. The three hours that followed were nightmares of exhausting action. There was no more running down hills and at the crest of each they stopped for long minutes. The heat had increased, and they dared not drink heavily lest cold water bloat them. When they struck a game trail, they followed it, but mostly there was dense underbrush that must be circled or crashed through and in the bottoms, alder bushes made almost impenetrable thickets.

Each hill had burgeoned hope of what might lie beyond, but each crest brought disappointment, so that Wentworth scarcely dared to gaze on the scenes below. The seventh hill seemed interminable; its crest was a bare ridge where rocks jostled the clouds. Twice, on the climb, Wentworth halted and June Calvert toiled to where he stood and went past him. The third time, he was just on the edge of the barren ridge that crowned the rise.

He stood there, gathering strength for the last pull, for the disappointment that must meet him from its top and once more June moved up beside him. Not even glancing in his direction, she traveled on heavily. Her stockings long ago had ripped from her legs and the flesh was torn and lacerated by thorns. Her head sagged so that her black hair half-hid her face and she moved with the steadiness, the stiffness of an automaton.

Wentworth watched her mount toward the crest; then he tramped on himself, head hanging, the white birch staff helping him up the grade. He did not look again at June, but abruptly he stopped, his down-gazing eyes seeing June upon her knees, head sagging, hands clasped together before her. He lifted his eyes and saw slow, blue smoke rising from the opposite slope of the hill. Was it already too late? He said nothing, but looked wearily at his watch. It was half-past four. If he could get a plane by six... It would take a half hour or more to reach that smoke.

He bent down and raised June to her feet and together, his arm supporting her, they went down the hill. The bottom was incredibly overgrown, but nothing could have stopped Wentworth now. He crashed through like a bull. On the far side, he stopped, peering upward. Laurel grew thickly ahead of him, screening the ground from view, but he could still see the smoke above the trees. What it portended, he did not know since there had been no house visible from the opposite ridge. But surely there were men here. They would be able to speed him on his way.

He turned, waited for June; then he pushed on again toward the laurel. He was looking at the ground when a rasping voice called out.

"You can stop right there, furriner!"

Wentworth glanced up sharply. A rifle muzzle yawned at him through a thick clump of laurel....

WENTWORTH LOOKED very calmly into the muzzle of the rifle. He had looked into similar eyes of death many times, but it was not that which calmed him now. It was his determination that nothing should stop him.

"Our plane crashed in a lake seven huts back," he said shortly. "I want a horse or some other means of getting to the nearest town. I'll pay for it... by check." He mentioned the method of payment as an afterthought. It would be very easy for the hidden man to shoot if he thought there was any chance for loot.

"We ain't got no hawses," he said flatly. "I reckon you better mosey back over them thar seven hills."

June Calvert was at Wentworth's shoulder. "Stop being a damned fool, Lemuel," she said. "We're not going back and you're going to help us to get out."

"Yuh know Lem?" another hidden man asked cautiously.

June Calvert said. "Oh, go to hell!" She walked to the right of the bushes where the rifle was poised. Wentworth was as puzzled as the rifleman obviously was, but he followed June. Two mountaineers came cautiously out of the laurel, tall, lanky, with squinting blue eyes.

"Where'd yuh ever meet up with Lem?" he demanded.

"I reckon I'll let Lem tell you that," June said steadily. "You tell him June Calvert said you were a damn'-sight faster with your rifle than you are with your brains. We want a flivver and we want it quick."

The older mountaineer blinked at June Calvert's words, moved his feet uncomfortably and spat tobacco juice at the hole of a tree.

"Wa'al," he mumbled, "if yuh know Lem, I reckon you be all right. We got a flivver over the hill a piece. You wantin' me to drive it?"

June shook her head, started up the hill. Wentworth followed her lead and the lanky mountaineer stood, with his arms folded over the muzzle of his rifle watching them go.

"Just leave the flivver at Pop Hawkins' store!" he yelled after them. "Tell him I'll be after it directly."

Wentworth felt the weariness drop from his legs. He went up the hill as freshly as he had started hours before. He ranged up beside June, glanced at her, curiously. Her lips were curved in a wide smile and she seemed hard put to choke back a laugh.

"You tricked him," Wentworth whispered wonderingly. "How in the world did you do it?"

They topped the hill before June spoke, then she laughed. "I used to teach school in the mountains," she said. "There isn't a family of them that hasn't got a Lemuel in it. If there wasn't

148

one in this family, the chances were that they knew somebody pretty well who had the name. It wasn't half as wide a shot as you might think. They've got a whiskey still on the hill. That's the reason for the rifle."

At the crest, Wentworth swept the valley beyond with a quick glance. It was fully five miles across and far down toward the north, was the smoke of a small town. But, best of all, there was a narrow, rutted road only a few hundred feet down. They went toward it rapidly.

"It was a very clever trick, June," Wentworth said. "I owe you one for that."

"You owe me nothing," June said sharply. "I was as much in danger as you were. What time is it?"

It was five minutes after five and Wentworth's lips drew tight and hard against his teeth as he hurried toward the ancient Ford that was parked in the middle of the road below. Wentworth had to crank it, but once started, the motor ran smoothly. He backed up a sharp embankment, wrenched the wheels about and sent it bounding down the steep hill.

THE ROAD twisted and wound between trees and rocks and bulging roots of trees. There were two ruts and between them grass grew. A more modern car would have scraped off its crank case in the first mile, but the high-wheeled Ford bounded as lightly as a goat from bump to bump and they made incredibly good time. Once a creek, which they forded, splashed water as high as the carburetor and almost stalled the engine, but it caught again and hurled them joyously down the valley.

Five miles of that and the road swung into a wider, dirt highway in which two cars could pass by running one wheel into the ditch. Three miles more and they came to a town of a dozen shacks with a general store labeled: "P. J. Hawkins, Merchandise, Groceries, Dry Goods, Seeds, Plows, etc." Wentworth jerked to a halt before it and went inside.

The town was Hawkinsville, Penn., and the railroad was twenty miles straight down the valley. Pop Hawkins wasn't sure whether there was an airport there, but there might be one at Pittsburgh. He said *Pittsburgh* as some people whisper *Heaven!* Yep, one of the boys did hire his car out sometimes. He went to the porch.

"Lem!" he shouted. "Lem Conley!" June, from the auto, winked at Wentworth. It was ten minutes before this Lemuel backed a wheezy Dodge from the stable and sent them rolling down the valley at a mad thirty-five miles an hour. Ordinarily, Wentworth would have enjoyed this out of the way corner of the world, but there was no time tor dalliance. It was close to six o'clock....

It was seven, and the sun was slanting toward the hills, when the Dodge wheezed up to the railway station of Dry Town. There would be no more trains that night. Airplanes? Well, now, over the hill there in Goochland County, they was having a fair and a fellow did some dad-fool stunts up in the air... No, 'twasn't fur, no more'n ten miles.

Wentworth almost despaired. He was dubious of the plane, too. Ships used for stunting would not be the racing type he would need if he were to reach Chicago before the Bat Man loosed his hordes upon Michigan City. But there was still a chance.

The Dodge labored up roads that seemed perpendicular, finally crested the mountain and swooped down into Goochland with bolts rattling like castanets. The aviator at the fair wheeled out an old Waco that would make ninety miles an hour in a pinch....

The red ball of the sun was balanced on the horizon and they took off into its eye. A half hour later, they set down at Pittsburgh and Wentworth chartered a fast Boeing, the only speedy job available on the field. Two hours from Chicago... and it was already deep twilight. How long before the Bat Man would release his murdering hordes?

Wentworth blindly watched the dark landscape sliding beneath the plane, the yellow lights of homes prick out. Those windows would be dark with death soon if the Bat Man were not overpowered.

Michigan City was the only hope of contact with him, and yet—did Wentworth have the right to risk the lives, nay to sacrifice lives, at the amusement park tonight so that he could meet once more with the Bat Man if he was not already too late. It was true that many hundreds would die if he did not find and kill the man, but was he justified? Was he not thinking more of the urgency of rescuing Nita and Jackson and Ram Singh, than of those thousands at the park tonight?

Wentworth's lips twitched, became ironically twisted. He got heavily to his feet and walked through the cabin to the cockpit.

There was only one pilot on this chartered trip and Wentworth dropped into the copilot's seat.

"Radio or wireless?" he questioned.

"Only wireless is working," the pilot yelled above the engine roar, "but I can send for you if you wish, sir."

WENTWORTH SHOOK his head and leaned forward to the key, began tapping out the call signals for Chicago police. He had been wrong, he acknowledged to himself, in delaying so long with the warning, but he had hoped against hope that he could reach the city before the fatal hour.

HXW, he called, HXW, until, closing the circuit, he heard the answering call, WT, HXW, WT, HXW. Then he began to pound out his warning, identifying himself first of all, for he was known to Chicago police also.

"Bat Man raiding Michigan City tonight with poison bats," he rapped out while the pilot glanced at him, admiring his sending fist. It was rapid, but clear and rhythmic, "Have information from escaped prisoner of Bat Man. Suggest that park be cleared instantly and information put on radio to keep windows shut, throughout city."

"Commissioner MacHugh sends thanks," the wireless buzzed back at him. "Will follow suggestion."

Wentworth signed off and switched off the set, leaned back in the seat with his eyes gazing off into the black sky. Well, it was done. He had thrown away the only chance he had of saving Nita from the death of the vampires. He argued with himself that he could not have behaved otherwise, but his heart felt cold when he lurched to his feet and stumbled back into the cabin.

June Calvert frowned at his white, drawn face. "What's the matter?" she demanded sharply.

Wentworth shook his head. No use in destroying her hopes of Jackson's rescue. Actually, he was despairing before there was need of it. It still was possible that the plane would reach Michigan City before the bats flew their lethal way through the night. He walked restlessly back and forth along the aisle of the ship, hands locked behind him. June caught his arm as he passed and stopped him.

"Something has gone wrong!" she said. "I know it."

Wentworth shrugged. "We'll be too late, you know that. The Bat Man will have attacked and gone before we get there."

"No." June protested, her dark face flushed despite the drain of fatigue. "He couldn't do that."

"Why not?"

"He just couldn't, not after the struggle we've put up. Why, things don't work out that way!" June was desperate.

Wentworth smiled at her wanly. "I hope you're right, June." He resumed his pacing. Abruptly, the door of the pilot compartment flung open. "Chicago police calling you," he shouted.

Wentworth ducked into the cockpit and fitted the headset to his ears again, waited until police had ceased signaling, then sent his answer winging through space, followed by a question.

Chicago's reply came with staccato speed. "Please repeat warning. Commissioner MacHugh, seven others in headquarters killed by bats."

Wentworth leaned forward tensely as he hammered out his message again. Chicago answered that Michigan City was in

153

hand, advised him to fly to Elgin, Illinois, and land at a field that would show a light. The Bat Man had been seen there, the police continued. Wentworth thanked them and signed off, but sat for a considerable while without ordering a change of course. An hour had rolled by and Columbus lay behind the plane. He turned to the pilot.

"Did that last sending seem the same tone, the same strength as the other?" he asked.

The pilot turned toward him, dropping the companion head-set that he wore about his neck. "Funny you should mention it," he said. "I had the same feeling about it—that it wasn't the same."

Wentworth's lips parted in a grim smile. "A decoy message, if I'm not mistaken," he said flatly. "Hold for Michigan City."

The pilot nodded cheerfully. "Yes, sir. Will there be a fight?"

"Pretty apt to be," Wentworth nodded. He got to his feet and started toward the cabin. He heard something hit with a rapid hammering thud just behind him, heard the pilot gasp and whipped about. The pilot was sagging forward over the controls, his head and body a mess of blood and across the twin windshields of the cockpit ran a stitching of bullet holes where machine gun lead had struck…!

CHAPTER 13
WHEN THE BATS FLY!

A N INSTANT after the discovery, Wentworth was hurled toward the front of the ship as it answered the pilot's push on the controls. Wentworth's lips moved with his furious curses as he fought to reach the co-pilot's seat. A glance at the altimeter showed him that he must move swiftly, for already the ship had plunged a thousand feet. The gauge showed nine hundred feet!

No need to wonder about the shooting. That decoy message actually had been used to trace his plane so that a killer from the Bat Man could locate him with a radio direction-finder and shoot him down. And it would have succeeded had he moved a moment later or a few minutes sooner. Had he left the cockpit, he could not have reached the controls in time and had he been later, the bullets would have sewn him to the seat as they had the pilot.

The altimeter read five hundred feet when Wentworth got his hand on the stick and began to ease it back. The ship continued to drop at terrific speed and the wings shook with the strain of his attempt to lever out of the dive. For long seconds, it seemed the mighty ship would plunge its engines into the earth, but finally the nose began to lift. Something scraped along the fuselage, tossed the ship wildly. Wentworth tripped off the lights, peered downward through the bullet-pocked windshield and saw the treetops just beneath. The plane's momentum pulled it through.

In a trice, it was zooming and Wentworth caught a glimpse of fiery exhaust blossoms high up in the heavens where the murder ship was circling to watch the finish of its work. Wentworth was grimly thankful that his own exhausts were muffled, so that his flight would not be detected. He made the big Boeing hop hedges for a dozen miles before he dared to let it surge upward toward the skies again. He had no means of defense but he thought it probable that he could outrace his attacker in a straight-away pursuit. He did not sight the plane again as he drove on his course toward Michigan City.

He could turn now to the pilot in the seat beside him, but there was nothing he could do there. The man had made no sound or movement since the bullets had drilled him. His breath had not even rattled in his throat. There could be no doubt he was dead. Wentworth's face was impassive, but there were cold fires of rage in his blue-gray eyes. Another man who served the Spider, even though briefly, had died. Was he forever to bring only death to those who helped him?

Grimly, he tugged the throttle of the ship wide until the motors were raving out there in the darkness and the propeller whine rose viciously. He must reach Michigan City before the Bat Man could strike and flee.

It occurred to Wentworth suddenly that June Calvert had made no sound since the shooting and he peered back into the cabin, saw her stretched on the floor with a bloody wound across her temple. It did not seem to be deep, but Wentworth could not leave the controls to investigate. He bent more tensely over the wheel.

Ahead of him was the glow of Michigan City, its thousand lights reaching up challengingly toward the sky. Still the radio did not speak of an attack there. Perhaps he was in time after all! He realized the ship was vibrating dangerously, as he continued to push it at peak speed, but he could not slacken off now.

Within fifteen minutes, he would be circling over the myriad lights....

THE RADIO squealed into action. "Calling all Michigan City cars. Calling Michigan City cars. Two men reported killed by bats in front of carousel. Car twenty-four investigate. Proceed with caution. All others stand by."

It had started then, this new mad murder-jag of the Bat Man. His warning had come too late....

He berated himself bitterly for his neglect, his selfishness in keeping the secret so long. Now Death would stride with seven-league boots across the park, taking great swaths of lives with each sweep of his keen scythe... Wentworth was directly over Michigan City now, swinging in great circles about its borders, searching for some trace of the Bat Man. He could see the bats, even from his height, clouds of fluttering killers. A touch on his shoulder startled him. He looked up into June Calvert's face. It was very pale and he knew that she had seen the pilot's body. The air made a keen hissing through the bullet holes that effec-tively prevented speech.

Twice more, Wentworth swung about the resort, then, suddenly, he spotted his enemy, the Bat Man. With great wings spread, he was gliding over the fleeing thousands who left many dead behind. With a great shout, Wentworth gunned the ship, put the nose down and dived directly on the Bat Man. If he struck him, the propellers would be ruined, motors would fly apart, death would hurl the ship downward. Wentworth knew those things, but it did not matter.

This black, gliding thing was the creature who had destroyed so many hundreds of lives, who had killed this brave man beside him, who had snatched Nita from his side. There was a snarling smile on the Spider's lips as, resolutely, he hammered downward at the Bat Man. Only two hundred feet from him, now only a hundred and fifty and the motors bellowed like hungry lions.

When Wentworth was only a hundred feet away, the Bat Man glided smoothly to the right. Wentworth wrenched the plane about in an effort to follow, but his momentum was too great. He shot on past the slowly moving man and plunged toward the milling crowds below. With a frantic effort, he pulled the great ship's nose upward, whirled it in a *virage* and darted to the attack again. He was handling the powerful Boeing as if it were a light pursuit ship and the wings quivered and vibrated, the engines labored.

THE BOEING dodged under the Bat's flight, whirled upward toward him with clawing propellers, the touch of which would slice the man in two. Wentworth had a glimpse of the drawn, frightened face of the Bat Man, saw a rifle spurt flame from near his head. He caught no bullet wind, but the man's effort pushed him just out of reach of the propellers, Savagely, Wentworth whirled the ship about and spotted the Bat Man fluttering downward like a wounded bird, sliding from side to side, whirling. Had he sliced the devil, then?

Wentworth took no chances. He sent the ship plunging toward the Bat Man, though they were now only two hundred feet above the earth. Even as he dived, he saw the Bat Man straighten out of his fall and speed earthward in a straight, controlled glide.

Grimly, Wentworth recognized that pursuit was now hope-less, for he saw the Bat Man glide downward between the high-reaching Ferris wheel and a switchback structure. No chance for the Boeing there, but he was quite sure the Bat Man could not wing his way upward again, Those wings would not provide him with enough lift for soaring. He whipped about toward June Calvert.

"I'm going to land on the beach," he rapped out. "Got to follow him. Go to the tail and strap yourself down."

June Calvert smiled slightly. "A parachute would be faster," she said. "I can handle the ship!"

Wentworth's smile was a cheer. He slipped out from behind the wheel and June Calvert took it with practiced hands. Within a minute, he was strapped into the parachute.

"Land it on the beach," he shouted at her, then went to the cabin door. He fought it open against the slip stream, crouched and dived below the tail group, snatched out the ring at once. June had shoved the ship upward, but the altitude was barely adequate. Wentworth landed heavily behind the switchback, sliced through the parachute shrouds with a keen pocket knife and raced for the open. He wore a flying helmet with goggles from the ship and his coat collar was turned high. Only the lower half of his face was exposed to the attacks of the bats, for his hands were gauntleted. Even so, he kept alert for the flying death.

It had been impossible to watch the landing of the Bat Man, but Wentworth had traced out his course and now he ran swiftly toward the spot his calculations indicated. He had

159

gone a hundred feet when a revolver spat from the darkness ahead. Wentworth fired at the flash and zig-zagged on. The revolver lanced flame at him again. Wentworth wasted no more shots. It was evident that the man who fired was behind some bullet-proof shield. For the Spider's lead always flew true to the target....

Twice more the revolver was fired and only once did the lead hum near. The man was a wretched shot, Wentworth thought. He raced on, heard his opponent flee crashingly through formal shrubbery that was planted nearby.

As he ran swiftly in pursuit, Wentworth saw that the man's shield had been a concrete bench. There was a strange odor of bat musk on the air and Wentworth's eyes were narrow. Certainly, the Bat Man did a thorough job of impersonation! He went lithely through the shrubbery, hurdled a hedge, raced along a gravel path....

OUT OF the darkness came the screams of men and women fleeing in panic before the bats. Wentworth owed his escape thus far from the poison vampires to the fact that all of the killers were hovering where the crowd was thickest. He realized this and saw, too, that the chase was leading directly toward the concourse of the amusement streets. Did the Bat Man then have some means of protection against his small assassins?

Changing his course, Wentworth ran parallel to the flight of his enemy. If he could outline him against the light from the thousand electric bulbs which still beckoned their invitation to the crowd there would be an immediate end to this slaughter. As if the fugitive guessed his purpose, he doubled back on his trail and fled again toward the formal garden and the switchback.

As they turned, Wentworth saw the huge Boeing slant to a landing on the sands. It bounced violently, but did not loop. Wentworth guessed that June Calvert had never before handled so large a ship, certainly not at night. She had courage! He had a new proof of that almost at once. The ship, once landed, did not remain stationary, but turned toward the park and trundled forward, its propellers lashing the air. June intended to shelter as many fugitives as possible in the cabin....

Now, at last, Wentworth caught a glimpse of the man he pursued. Good lord, the Bat Man still wore his wings! Wentworth flung lead after him, saw him trip and fall. A great shout welled out of the Spider's throat. He dashed forward, then abruptly, flung himself flat to the earth also. From the shadows ahead came the liquid pop of blowguns. The Bat Man had led him into an ambush!

Wentworth lifted his head and grimly leveled his automatic. He realized that the Indians were moving rapidly to surround him. They would close in slowly until sure that the Spider was dead. He had eleven cartridges and there were easily thirty Indians...!

CHAPTER 14
IN THE BAT'S TRAP

THE FEELING of despair that had never been far from Wentworth's heart since the first battle against the Bat

Man surged over him again, but it received a sudden check. Unbidden, without preliminary, the thought rose in Wentworth's mind: *Nita is not dead!* And there was a reason for the thought. The Bat Man had not had time to go to more than one bat depot—and the bats of that group must be kept hungry for the night's attack! No, Nita had not yet been fed to the vampires.

With the thought, Wentworth felt a flood of new vigor come into him. If Nita lived, he would save her, despite this ambush of poison darts. There was one way... They would not begin to close in until they had completed the circle about him and there was yet an opening of twenty feet in the rear. Wentworth made no move toward it. Instead, he rapidly began to wriggle out of the parachute harness from which he had sliced the shrouds, rather than discard it in his need for speed.

He gouged out a deep hollow the ground, set the butt of his gun in it and packed the earth down tightly about it. He fastened an end of the parachute harness, whose straps he had cut to stretch it to the greatest possible length, to the trigger of the automatic and the other end he held in his hand as he crawled straight toward where the Bat Man had fallen!

When he had gone a few feet, he pulled gently on the harness until the automatic fired. He smiled grimly. He was giving the poison darts a target, but it was a false one.

The rain of darts increased behind him as he crawled to the attack. There were four shots in the automatic. They lasted him twelve feet, half the distance to the Bat Man. He tried then to drag the empty pistol to him but the strap slipped loose and he was compelled to abandon it. To return there through the fire of the Indians would be fatal. Besides, the circle was complete and the blowgun men were beginning to close in. Unarmed, he pushed rapidly on.

The innocuous seeming pop of the deadly guns sounded strange against the background of panic screams out there where the bats were thick. Through the middle of sound, he caught, too, a distant rumble as of a train. Were police coming by rail? But that was foolish... He realized abruptly that the sound came from the switchback where cars were running wild, empty, about the tracks, abandoned by the operators who had fled, or been killed by the bats. The scent of bat musk was heavy all about him.

ALREADY, WENTWORTH could make out the black hump that marked where the Bat Man lay. The sight tightened his mouth, narrowed his eyes to a steely hardness. He was only six feet away—now only three! He hunched himself up on tense thighs, hurled himself bodily upon the middle of the wings! He fell on fabric. A metal brace prodded him in the side, but that was all. *The Bat Man was gone!*

The sound of Wentworth's leap had not passed unnoticed. While he lay, half-dazed by his fall, an Indian called in a nasal shout that was a challenge. Wentworth could not answer. He did not know the language. A bat-like squeak in the wrong tone might be equally betraying. But there was a way out. He thrust himself to one side of the brace which evidently supported the wings, got to the edge of the queer contraption and crawled underneath it. His lips were smiling. Even the light fabric of the wings would be enough to protect him from the darts if the Indians dared to fire at the spot where their master had been!

Wentworth began to wriggle along flat on his stomach, carrying the wings with him. His acute ears heard the advance of the blowguns as their popping grew louder. When they were almost upon him, he halted. When they passed, he began again the slow crawling. Fifteen feet outside of their circle, he slid out from under the wings and, bent double, raced away on silent feet.

Where had the Bat Man gone? Wentworth found himself sprinting toward the high, spidery structure of the switchback. There, he could escape the Indians.

Under its shadows he crept, and crouching there, he became aware again of that strange, over-powering scent of bat musk which he had detected earlier in the night. He twisted his head about, sniffing like a dog. Unless he was fooled by the wind, the scent was stronger toward his left. Without hesitation, Wentworth crept in that direction. The Bat Man was armed and the Spider was empty-handed, but it would have taken more than that to turn him back tonight!

The scent was stronger now. Wentworth crouched low, seeking to outline his enemy against the sky but there were only the stilts of the switchback. He pushed on. The scent grew fainter. He pivoted back again, frowning in perplexity, angry in frustration. Then there was an infinitesimal squeak, as of leather on wood, almost directly above him. He tilted back his head and saw, outlined like a spider in a squared web of wood against the sky, a man climbing among the braces of the switchback. STRANGLING DOWN the cry of triumph that rose in his throat, Wentworth sprang to a horizontal brace just above his head, and swung up, clambered to his feet. The structure was built with high verticals and horizontals like the floor of a house. Then in each oblong made by the crossing of uprights and cross-pieces, there were X-braces, stretched diagonally from corner to corner. It was a simple matter to walk up one of these diagonals, using the crosspieces as a handrail. Wentworth clambered swiftly in the wake of the little man who was making panicky speed for the top.

Wentworth recognized the Bat Man's plan. At the top of the first incline toward which the man climbed, the cars moved at a snail's pace. It would be an easy matter for him to climb in and sail over the runways to safety before Wentworth could overtake him. There was one defect in his plan. He could get out only at the spot where he had entered, on the long initial incline up which the cars were drawn by a chain—unless one of his hench-men could operate the brakes which ordinarily stopped the cars, but which were independent of the cars themselves.

The Bat Man was half-way to the top now, climbing like a monkey among the cross-braces. Wentworth was fully thirty feet below him. He abandoned walking the X-braces and started scrambling up them like a ladder, X-brace to crosspiece, to X-brace again. It was dizzying work and every second increased the distance above the ground and the peril. Out there in the darkness, the flying cars squealed on curves or rumbled down inclines that were almost perpendicular. At the bottom of the incline, a car was beginning its clanking rise to the peak which the fugitive sought.

Wentworth realized with a despairing cry that the Bat Man would reach the top in time to board the car, and that he himself could not. He threw a sharp, estimating glance about as he fought upward at top speed. The rails of first dip were only about half the distance of the top from him, and to walk the crosspieces to it would take only seconds. The string of cars, four hitched together, would be gaining the momentum for its entire run there, but the point opposite Wentworth was less than half way down the swoop. It would be accelerating—not yet at its peak speed....

Grimly, swiftly as always, the Spider made his choice. Already, he was footing it along the cross-piece. He reached the track before the car arrived at the top of the incline where the Bat Man was even now scrambling. While there was yet time, Wentworth scrambled ten feet higher along the track. Then he crouched and waited for the car. There was a railing here and he poised on its top, which would be barely on a level with the side of the car seats. It would be a perilous undertaking!

Wentworth's jaw locked rigidly, the muscles in his thighs tautened... The cars had reached the crest. The Bat Man scrambled in and, with a rising roar, the train plunged down the rise toward where Wentworth waited.

The Bat Man saw him, raised up in the front seat with his revolver in his hand and a despairing cry in his throat. There would be a split-second when he was directly opposite Wentworth—when he could shoot at him at point-blank range. He would, at that time, be moving at about thirty miles an hour. Wentworth estimated his chances, crouching there on the rail, and his lips drew back from his teeth. The cars roared toward him...!

WENTWORTH WAS not standing broadside to the cars, but was facing the same direction in which they were traveling. He had no way of estimating the velocity of his leap, but it could not reasonably be more than fifteen miles an hour. That difference was enough to make it damnably dangerous. Added to that was the fact that his footing, both in jumping and landing, was extremely uncertain. He did not need that threatening revolver to make it a life-and-death attempt. He must spring into the air at exactly the right heart-beat of time. There must be no hesitation, no slip-up.

And yet, as the car hurtled toward him, Wentworth flung his laughter into the air—reckless, taunting laughter. The Bat Man leaned forward, stretching the revolver out before him. He was almost upon Wentworth.

"Lookout, fool!" Wentworth shouted.

His cry was at just the right moment. It caught the Bat Man squeezing the trigger—the front of the car almost level with Wentworth. At the same instant, Wentworth jumped. If he could, he meant to hammer the Bat Man to the floor with the bludgeon of his body. But he miscalculated—either his own speed or that of the train—for his feet caught on the back of the cushion of the third car. The blow smacked his feet out from under him and hurled him, headfirst, into the seat of the fourth car.

The car whirled sickeningly around a curve, jamming Wentworth over against one side of the seat; then it straightened out for another dive. The rush of wind helped to clear Wentworth's brain and he thrust stiff arms into the cushions, shoved himself erect. He was almost thrown out as the car plunged again. He peered ahead, saw the glint of a revolver and pulled his head down as the bullet whined.

The Spider still did not have complete control over his body, but there was no time to be lost. The moments when he could crawl forward to the attack were terribly limited, for the track led under the cross-braces of other tracks and to stand up would mean a broken neck. Likewise, the sideways of the U-turns would hurl him off by centrifugal force.

Nevertheless, Wentworth set himself grimly to climb forward. He jerked the cushion from the seat and, when next there was an instant of clear overhead, he hurled it forward against the blast of the wind and threw himself head first into the third car of the train.

The cushion did not reach the first car, but it had made the Bat Man duck and before he could shoot, Wentworth was under cover—one car nearer the front! He thought that the next cushion he hurled would reach its goal.

Already, the train was starting the last and lowest circuit of the structure. Wentworth realized that he would have no further chance to advance on his enemy until a new circuit was started. Meantime, the Bat Man would have the long, slow climb up the incline in which to escape. His hands clenched with determination as he crouched behind the protection of the car's front. If the Bat Man attempted to get off this car, he would have the Spider on his back!

"If you jump out," Wentworth called to him, "I'm going to push you off. I won't have to touch you. A cushion...."

Wentworth did not again lift his head above the seats, but he leaned far over to the side and peered toward the front car. He saw a foot thrust out cautiously. He started to shout a warning to the man to get back, but shut his mouth grimly and held his cushion ready. The Bat Man's foot reached out farther. They were almost to the top and he must hurry if he was to get away before that. Wentworth saw the foot lift a little and hurled the cushion.

The heavy combination of wood and leather struck the walk-way beside the track just as the Bat Man stepped down, hit the same place. The Bat Man screamed, lost his footing and fell flat. He rolled against the side of the car, bounced toward the low guard railing. Wentworth sprang to his feet to hurl himself upon the man, but at that moment the car gave a lurch and surged over the top of the incline!

Wentworth cursed, peered back and saw the Bat Man roll onto the tracks which the car had just quitted, then the train carrying Wentworth whipped down into that first, terrific dip. The Spider sat and cursed under his breath the entire way around the switch-back. The circuit that last time had been so swift—stretched out interminably—but at last the train swept toward the chained incline. Wentworth sprang out, peered eagerly upward and—*The Bat Man was gone!*

Both the Bat Man and the Indians had vanished. Heavily, he turned toward the plane, and while he went, by back-ways where the bats were not, he heard the piercing, gigantic squeaking which he knew was the recall signal for the vampires. There was no tracing the sound. It seemed to come from everywhere....

Wentworth broke into a run. The battle was not yet lost. If

169

all roads were blocked and all small men detained for examination… At the plane, he found a group of uniformed police and, inside their circle, Commissioner MacHugh, of Chicago, was shooting questions at June Calvert.

June was taking it languidly, leaning against the side of the Boeing with a glint of humor in her dark eyes. She had taken advantage of the interim to fluff her black hair about the piquant oval of her face. But her beauty was only a mask for grim determination. That much, Wentworth knew.

HE THRUST through the circle after MacHugh had identified him. MacHugh was small, but he had a big, hearty manner. His energy was tiring to watch. He sprang forward to grasp Wentworth's hand. "By all that's holy, Wentworth!" he shouted. "I was about to string the girl up by her thumbs because she wouldn't talk. How do you pick 'em, my boy? How do you pick 'em?"

Wentworth grinned into the Commissioner's face. The man was infectious. "Commissioner, the Bat Man was here just a few minutes ago. I fought with him, but he got away. I suggest that we stop all roads and search for small men, not above a hundred pounds…."

MacHugh made a move. His complexion was dark and his frown made his face ugly. "I escape by one pound! Is the Bat Man small?"

"He is," Wentworth said grimly. "After all the small men are together, I want to look them over. There's a bare chance I might identify him."

"I say, there, Commissioner Mac Hugh!" a man's voice piped.

Wentworth spun about to stare beyond the circle of police. He caught his breath. Sanderson, the weazened ex-jockey turned stable owner, was just outside the cordon, waving at MacHugh.

"Let him in," the Commissioner called. He turned to Wentworth. "Sanderson came out with me. We were at a show and just got here a few seconds ago. Sanderson wanted to look about."

Wentworth stared suspiciously at Sanderson as the little man sauntered up, swaggering a bit. His mind was racing. Both of these men were small—both had just arrived on the scene. Was it possible that… one of these men was the Bat?

Wentworth moved to June's side, turning his back on the others.

"When the big squeak was made," be whispered, "was MacHugh here?"

June shook her head, glanced over his shoulder at the commissioner. "Do you think…?"

Wentworth shrugged. "I don't know," he said, suddenly weary. Once more, the Bat Man had won… There was no longer any need to starve the bats. Nita, dear Nita….

CHAPTER 15
A CLUE AT LAST

A DRAGGING weariness rode with Wentworth back to Chicago in Commissioner MacHugh's sedan. He sat on a kick seat beside Sanderson, who kept up a half-apologetic conversation on the horrors he had seen at Michigan City. The dead were estimated at three thousand, five hundred.

"Some of them must have suffered horribly," Sanderson went on in his subdued voice. "One boy had strangled a bat in each hand, but he had at least a dozen bites on his face and neck. I picked up a bat, and ever since then, I fancy I smell like the damned things."

Wentworth said nothing, but his thoughts were swift. Now that Sanderson had called attention to it, he did catch a faint whiff of the bat-musk which had been so powerful in the vicinity of the Bat Man. Suspicion leaped full-grown into his brain. It wasn't possible that bat scent should cling so to a person who had only handled a dead one. He decided that Sanderson's movements should be watched, his whereabouts at other appearances of the Bat Man checked.

Where did the scent that the Bat Man used come from? Surely, not from merely handling bats, nor from the glands of the bat itself. To generate such a powerful taint of it, hundreds of bats would have to be slaughtered and certainly, the Bat Man could not have a great enough supply of bats to warrant such butchery. Only one explanation was possible then. The scent was artificial, and....

Wentworth sat abruptly straight, spun toward MacHugh. "Commissioner, will you have your men gather every dead bat possible at the park and rush them to me at the Blackstone hotel? This is important! It may mean the solution of the case!"

Sanderson shuddered. "I should hope so. Vampires! Brrrr!"

Fatigue and mental fag lifted from Wentworth's body. At last he had a trail which might lead to the Bat Man. And it was one that could be followed swiftly... He engaged a suite of rooms at the Blackstone and, one hour after the dead bats had been delivered to him there, he left with June Calvert for the airport. The Boeing had been refueled and new windows substituted for those the machine gun had wrecked. At Wentworth's orders, these were bullet proof. The pilot was a United States marine officer whose mouth was straight and pugnacious below a pointed nose. His eyes were direct.

"What the hell's up? And who are you?" he demanded when Wentworth entered.

Wentworth smiled slightly. He mentioned his title and regiment of the reserves, his name. The Marine came sharply to his feet, saluted with a crisp efficiency.

"Begging the major's pardon," he said flatly, "but they got me up out of the first night's sleep I've had in a week. Lieutenant Carlisle, sir."

"At ease," Wentworth told him briefly.

"I asked for a pilot without nerves, who was reasonably good with an automatic and better than good as to courage. I'm satisfied. Take off at once. All possible speed for the Rocky Mountains, about fifty miles south of Hooligan Pass."

The lieutenant saluted, fairly jumped to the controls. The plane swept down the field, lofted gently and swung about in a bank that almost scraped off the wingtip.

WENTWORTH'S FACE was drawn with harsh lines of fatigue. There were dark smudges beneath his eyes, a deeper crease at his mouth corners.

"We're going to the Bat Man's main headquarters," he said

shortly. "The purpose is to kill him and save certain persons who are his prisoners."

"But how do you know where to go?" June demanded.

Wentworth smiled faintly. "I've got a good nose. I'm going to sleep."

It was not the least of Wentworth's miracles that he could sleep when all his soul and body stirred with anxiety. But there was nothing he could do now, and how many hours had it been since he had last slept…? Two hours after the takeoff, Wentworth sprang up from the cushions. Many of the lines had been erased from his face and, after a swift toilet, he was fresh, and vigorous. He went into the cockpit, dropped into the co-pilot's seat.

"Mr. Carlisle," he said, "We're going to kill the Bat Man."

The lieutenant turned his head briefly. "Yes, sir."

"Do you know the Rockies, Mr. Carlisle?"

"Yes, sir."

Wentworth smiled faintly.

"Interrupt me if I'm wrong, Mr. Carlisle," he said. "About fifty miles south of Hooligan Pass, there is a section in which hot springs abound. Also, due to the action of this hot water upon limestone, there are large, far-reaching caverns. In the recesses of those caves, it is likely that the heat—due to the water— would approximate that of the tropical river regions of South America where vampire bats live. In those caves, vampire bats could breed just as they do in the tropics and thus produce the overwhelming numbers which have been loosed on America. Do you agree with me that far, Mr. Carlisle?"

"Yes, sir!" There was a rising enthusiasm in the lieutenant's voice.

"How long, Mr. Carlisle, before we'll reach that section?"

"Twenty-two minutes, sir!" Wentworth nodded and got to his feet. "I am looking for a canyon in that district into which it would be impossible to descend, Mr. Carlisle. Signal me when you reach Hoot-Owl Center."

Wentworth returned to the cabin and found June Calvert sitting up sleepily. He crossed to a long paper-wrapped package that he had picked up in Chicago, which had been brought from New York by plane. He unwrapped it quickly and revealed a pair of wings, folded flat together. June sprang to her feet.

"The Bat Man's wings!" she cried. Wentworth shook his head. "No, mine," he said, "but modeled after the Bat Man's. Because of my greater weight, I had to increase their size. Will you help me, please?"

HE LIFTED the wings and adjusted the straps over his shoulders. The wings folded flat together and pointed out rigidly some nine feet along the cabin. There were straps also about waist and ankles to support his body. When he jumped from the plane, a jerk would snap the wings out to each side and lock them there. A kick would move the rudder into position just behind his feet. There were tip aerolons which he could operate by twisting his wrists and his feet rested on the rudder rod. There was no elevator. The aerolons and the shifting of his body would take care of dives. There would be little climbing.

June Calvert looked at him with wide eyes. "But why, why?" she whispered.

Wentworth laughed. "Didn't the Bat Man say no one but himself could reach his hide-out unless he willed it? Well, I am now the Bat Man so far as aerial navigation is concerned!"

From up forward came a queer hooting sound and for a moment, Wentworth did not identify it. Then he realized its meaning. Lieutenant Carlisle had signaled that the ship was over Hoot-Owl Center. Wentworth smiled slightly as he released himself from the straps, leaned the wings against the wall and walked forward. The little mountain town lay beneath them and ahead lifted the barrier of the Rockies. A small, crooked road wove its way upward into the fastness and on it Wentworth made out three auto trains of seven or eight cars apiece. His eyes narrowed at the sight and he caught up a pair of field glasses and focused them on the road.

The cars were trucks and each carried big boxes that would be far too heavy a load for the vehicles if they contained weighty cargo. Furthermore, the men who manned the trucks were Indians, not the lithe, red men of the North American wilderness, but the stubby, fierce savages from the Amazon, each with his blowgun.

Wentworth's hand dropped on the pilot's shoulder. "These are the men of the Bat," he said. "Climb as high as possible while still keeping an eye on them. See where they go, and then I have some twelve-pound bombs."

Lieutenant Carlisle said, "Yes, sir!"

Wentworth strode sharply back into the cabin with elation singing in his veins.

June Calvert stood up and moved toward him. "What is it?"

she demanded, whispering. She had to repeat the words before Wentworth looked at her.

"We're close now," he said. "Very close." He moved toward the wings that were shaped like a bat's.

Carlisle's voice rang out from the cockpit, "Major!"

Wentworth hurried to him.

"They've stopped, sir," Carlisle said. "They're getting out."

Wentworth took the glasses and peered down. The plane had climbed three thousand feet, but was still easily visible to the men below. Their flattish faces were turned upward. Wentworth's lips thinned. He lowered the glasses.

"They've guessed we're following! Bomb them. Drop down to fifteen hundred. I'll throw the bombs out of the door."

Carlisle spun the ship about and Wentworth dragged out two wooden cases from opposite walls of the cabin, opened them and took out two bombs shaped like tear drops, but with fins on the tails to keep their nose down. He forced open the door and waited while the Boeing circled downward. Wentworth could see the upturned faces without glasses now. He held the bombs ready.

June Calvert came and stood beside the box. "I'll hand them to you," she said.

THE THREE motorcades had merged and were strung out along the road for over a half-mile. Wentworth waited until the ship was in position, then darted the first bomb toward the head of the line. It struck ten feet to the side of the road and splintered a huge pine. The second bomb made a direct hit on the second truck. The body went to pieces. The big cages of bats were tossed a hundred feet and the steel frame soared and crushed the front of the fifth truck in line.

The Boeing zoomed, viraged and swept back over the road again. Indians were scattering in all directions from the trucks, blocked permanently the by the first bomb Wentworth had thrown. The last truck was trying frantically to turn about and retreat. Wentworth's third bomb hit close by, dug a pit under its wheels and flopped the car over on its side. Systematically then, Wentworth pelted the rest of the trucks until not one remained undamaged.

"One of the trucks got away," June told him tensely. "The first one in line. You missed it and it went up into the mountains."

Lieutenant Carlisle evidently had noticed it, too. The ship was sent hurtling after the truck, but Wentworth put his last two bombs back into the case, went forward to the cockpit.

"Keep the truck in sight," he ordered.

There was a drumming thud upon the roof of the cabin. The hammering moved forward and in its wake appeared a seam of bullet holes. A machine gun! Wentworth cursed. He pulled June Calvert far back into the tail of the ship, saw the windows of the cockpit sliver under the hail of lead, but resist the attack. The tail of the ship whipped over, wind roared in through the open door as Carlisle put the giant Boeing into a side-slip to dodge the attacking plane.

The bomb case lurched toward the opening and, even as Wentworth darted forward to seize it, plunged outward into space. The roar of wind through the door abruptly checked and Wentworth knew the Boeing was sliding in the opposite direction. He saw a jot of earth leap upward where the bomb case struck. The road was blocked! That accidental discharge of high explosive had struck squarely in the middle of the mountain trail and dug a twenty foot pit across it. And the truck they were following was on the far side of that pit!

Now there would be no trail to lead them to the headquarters of the Bat Man. They would have to guess at its location... Wentworth shouted forward. "Turn your port side to the plane!"

The Boeing zoomed, whirled in a vertical bank and, peering upward now through the open door, Wentworth had a glimpse of a speedy little monoplane diving toward him. There was a flicker of flame behind the propeller that showed his machine guns....

"Up!" Wentworth shouted.

He felt the plane lift even as the machine gun fire dipped. The bullets missed... The ship was close enough now. No need to aim. Wentworth held both automatics on the nose of the ship, held on the face of the man just visible behind the windshield of the attacking plane. He pumped the full charge of both automatics.

THE MONOPLANE zoomed, fell off on the left wing and screamed downward in a whipping, screaming tail-spin. Wentworth, stepping back from the doorway to reload his automatics, could see the pilot lolling helplessly back against the crash pad. The Spider's eyes narrowed as his lips parted in a smile. The man was dead. That much was obvious, but was it the Bat Man? Grimly, he hoped that it was, but he doubted such luck. The Bat Man usually made his attacks on his own wings....

Wentworth slipped the loaded weapons back into his holsters and pushed forward. There was nothing to do now but follow the road and hope that they would be able to spot a canyon that might fit the description Wentworth had given. He dropped in the co-pilot's seat and waited while the Boeing made slow wide circles over wild, mountain country.

A squealing sound, not unlike the squeak of a giant bat, came from the wireless head-phones and Wentworth, frowning, lifted them to his ears. The squealing continued, but now it was broken into short and long sounds. Wentworth cursed, pressed the phones closer… It was Morse code! Swiftly, Wentworth deciphered the message:

"Unless you at once return the way you came," ran the dots and dashes, "you will forfeit the lives of three friends and the woman you love. Furthermore, I shall shoot you down, as I am in a position to do at this moment. Consider, Spider, the lives of four people against a strategic retreat. Which do you choose?"

The squealing stopped for a moment, then began again, the same message. Coolly, Wentworth moved the coil of the radio direction-finder. "Two points east of north," he said to Carlisle, "and very near. He is threatening to shoot us down. Keep a sharp eye out for attacking planes."

Wentworth moved hurriedly back into the cabin then and donned the wings, tightening all the straps. Just short of the tip aerolons, there were two holsters and into these, Wentworth thrust his automatics. He stood by the door, peering down at the mountains sliding past below him.

Carlisle shouted, "Plane is attacking ahead, Major. Something funny... Good God, *it's the Bat Man!*"

Wentworth turned about and smiled at June Calvert. "Tell Carlisle to dodge the plane and circle aloft. He'll have the ceiling of that monoplane. Tell him to look for a signal from that canyon we're passing over."

June Calvert nodded, staring at him with wide eyes. Wentworth shouted forward, "When I shout, kick the tail to starboard!"

"Yes, sir!"

Wentworth paused in the doorway, gazing downward, his hands moved over the buckles of the wings that jutted oddly from his shoulders. There was a grim, drawn tension about his mouth. He poised in the doorway like a diver, shouted at Carlisle, then sprang head foremost into space, with only those queer wings and his skill to save him from inevitable death on the rocks five thousand feet below...!

CHAPTER 16
THE JAWS OF DEATH

WENTWORTH PLUNGED downward at terrific speed, falling free, the wings of no more value than a tangled parachute. He spread his legs so that the fin between them straightened, the rudder whipped back into position. He was falling headfirst now and it was easy to pull the wings about into flying station.

He twisted the aerolons, kicked the rudder and immediately

felt the lift of the wings. He shot forward on a level with the momentum of his plunge, peered about and a shout of anger and hate rang out. The Bat Man was diving headfirst toward the Boeing and, even as Wentworth shouted, the giant plane faltered, slid off on one wing and nosed down. It took only a glance to realize that the Bat Man's rifle bad penetrated the bulletproof glass and that the Marine pilot and June Calvert were plunging to their death!

Instinctively, as Wentworth saw what had happened, he tilted back his aerolons and zoomed up toward the Bat Man. It was not until then that the man saw Wentworth, flying on wings so like his own. When he did, he staggered uncertainly for a moment, his flying speed falling off. Instantly, he overcame his surprise and dived to gather momentum.

It was only then that Wentworth realized the difficulty of the thing he had undertaken. He had intended the wings to enable him to penetrate the Bat's hiding place, now suddenly, he found himself forced to fight in a field in which his opponent was easily the master. He was plunged instantly into a life and death struggle!

Wentworth realized these things when he prolonged his zoom too long in an effort to gain altitude on the Bat Man. He lost flying speed, whip-stalled and found himself plunging for the earth at a furious pace. Aerolons and rudder kicked him out of it, but he found the Bat Man sweeping toward him nose-on. The rifle which Wentworth now saw was strapped to the top of the wing and was aligned with the man's body. It spat flame and a bullet whipped past within inches of his head.

Wentworth's face was grimly set. If the Bat Man expected any armament at all, he would naturally conceive it to be of the same type of his own. Actually, Wentworth's automatics were pointed straight out to each side, slung in holsters through whose tip they could fire as readily as if held freely in the hands. As Wentworth wheeled out of the line of fire, he pointed a wingtip toward the Bat Man and squeezed the trigger. The recoil kicked the wing upward slightly and Wentworth had to twist aerolons to straighten out his curious craft. The bullet went wide.

Wentworth completed a circle but found the Bat Man had the speed of him, from his dive. His enemy shot about in an almost vertical bank which Wentworth would have believed impossible and the rifle was leveled once more. A bullet from the Bat Man's rifle struck the wing and tugged at Wentworth's sleeve. A second shot close on its heels, struck the duralumin brace and whined off into space.

Wentworth dived. It was the only thing he could do. The Bat Man followed and the Spider saw that he had one advantage—speed of descent. In a vertical plunge of course, both would drop at the same pace, but at a glide, Wentworth's greater weight, his higher ratio of weight to wing spread gave him the advantage. But he could not out-fly bullets....

LEAD CRACKED over his head viciously. Wentworth kicked the rudder and dodged. He repeated that while bullets sang and whined about him. The wing was struck again. Wentworth twisted his head about and saw the Bat Man was gaining on him slightly because of his dodging. As he looked, the squealing, rasping signal that was a call to the bats rang out. Good lord, was the man summoning the vampires to his assistance?

Wentworth whipped about and tried once more to down the man with automatic shots, but his lack of lateral control handicapped him badly. He dared not empty his guns with such poor assurance of success and he was forced once more to turn and run. The Spider run from an enemy! It was incredible, but it was so. The man had greater skill.

They were dangerously close to earth now. No more than a thousand feet. Wentworth continued to dodge while he searched the earth with eager eyes. Over to his right was the deep slit of a canyon. Beneath him, all was dense woods. There was no spot to mark where the Boeing had crashed. Desperately, Wentworth searched the earth for some spot in which to land. There was none.

Abruptly, Wentworth remembered the reason for his wings. They had been for the purpose of entering the secret hiding place of the Bat Man, of invading the canyon cave in which, Wentworth deduced, he had made his headquarters. There was a canyon, and the attack upon him had been begun near it. He would have to chance a dive into its tricky and turbulent wind currents.

With his mind made up, Wentworth slanted directly for the darkened mouth of the canyon. Behind him, the Bat Man screamed again and it seemed to Wentworth that it was more than a signal. The sound held a touch of fright, perhaps of anger. The Bat pressed him more closely, dived steeply to intercept his approach to the cliffs. Wentworth smiled thinly. He had guessed right then. The hiding place was there! He would enter that canyon or die in the attempt.

The Bat pressed closer, closer, his rifle barking again and again. Wentworth watched him come with worried, angry eyes. There was death for one of them here on the lip of the cliffs, or in that narrow bit of air that led downward into the throat of the canyon itself. In that confined space, there could be little dodging, little hope of escape. Bullets would fly....

On the point of darting downward into the canyon, Wentworth whipped upward into a zoom almost head on toward the Bat Man. He twisted the aerolons and side-slipped toward the valley below. As he slipped, holding his wings steadily vertical so that he plunged at terrific force toward the stony death below, he began to shoot. For the first time, now, in that perilous position, he had the stability he needed for accuracy. His first shot caught the right wing of the Bat Man. His second plucked at the man's clothing. But in his steady dive, Wentworth exposed himself to the fire of his enemy's rifle and the bullets whipped closer, closer....

A knife of fire slit down Wentworth's right arm and his hand went utterly numb and useless. He knew that one of the bullets had touched him at last. It was a superficial wound, but it might well mean death! The crippling of that arm loosened one of the aerolons to flap as it would. It halved his armament...!

A WILD challenging shout rang from the Spider's lips. Its echo battered at him from both walls of the canyon, but it seemed to him that there was another shriller voice shouting, too. He fought grimly to hold on with his numb hand to the handle of the aerolon. He did not seek to use it, merely to hold it stationary while with his other hand and the rudder he maneuvered his other wing uppermost. As the rudder turned him, first, head-down, then over again, he caught a glimpse of a black cave's mouth far below and, on the ledge before it, several figures stood with arms uplifted. By the gods, if that Bat Man did not kill the Spider in the air, then the man's Indians would slaughter him when he landed!

Bitterly, Wentworth completed his whirl, thrust his gun-hand upward. If he died, he at least would not die alone!

His hands moved, his feet kicked the rudder. Before his eyes whirled the black opening of the cave he had seen and the gesturing figures. They were going to kill him, were they? He tried to kick a wing about so that he could shoot, but he forgot to bank or his hands failed on the aerolons when he did it. He skated sideways, twisting his head about to see the death that presently would strike into him.

In God's name, who was this who held out waiting arms to him? That face! Nita! *Good God. Nita!* He felt that he was still skidding sideways toward that lovely face that floated before his eyes. He saw men leap toward him, then... nothing!

Impossible to tell whether he was unconscious for an hour or a second, but the crooning of Nita's voice drifted away and returned to him in waves of sound. He pushed his eyes open, looked up into Nita's face. He struggled up....

"The Bat Man! The Bat Man!" he cried. "Where is he?"

"Dead, darling," Nita told him. "You shot him down out in

the canyon there, before you side-slipped into a landing here on the ledge."

Wentworth moved his arms stiffly and found a biting pain in the right one, found the left unencumbered by the wing. He looked about him. June Calvert was standing near, with Jackson's arm about her. Fred Stoking and Ram Singh smiled at him. The Marine lieutenant....

"Mr. Carlisle," Wentworth said weakly, "How in the hell do you happen to be still alive?"

The Marine grinned. "I faked out-of-control and landed in the canyon valley. There's a rope ladder up here. Had quite a tussle with some of those vampire bats up here. They came out when that guy screamed up there in the air, but they couldn't see in the daylight very well and we got the best of them."

Wentworth sank back on the hard rock of the ledge gratefully. "Well, Earl Westfall will never be electrocuted then."

Nita smiled at him, "How did you know the Bat Man was Westfall? We found out when we came here that he wasn't the fat man he seemed at all. He had a rubber suit that he blew up. It made him look huge. And that Bat Man face of his—it was a mask."

Wentworth looked about, found June Calvert's eyes. "You ought to know how I found out, how I learned where the headquarters was."

JUNE CALVERT shook her head. "I haven't the faintest idea," she said happily, "but I don't see that it matters much as long as you did." She looked up into Jackson's wide, grinning face.

"Really," Wentworth complained, "won't somebody inquire how the great Wentworth learned the secret?"

Nita laughed and brushed his forehead with her lips. "Tell me, darling," she whispered. "I'll always want to know."

"The bat musk secret," Wentworth said. "None of the Indians was ever attacked by the bats and there had to be a reason. It was because they smelled like bats."

They were interested now, all of them. Fred Stoking looked at Nita with wistful, but hopeless, eyes.

"It wasn't possible for the Bat Man—or Westfall—" Wentworth went on, "to get enough bat glands to make the odor, so he had to make it artificially. The bat musk was strangely like some perfume I had run across. Basically, of course. I identified the perfume—Chatou's Oriental—and found out where large shipments of it had been made. It came to Hoot-Owl Center, and would you believe it? Westfall actually had it addressed to his stable manager! But I had been suspicious of Westfall for some time. I found out from some of my newspaper clippings that he had recently been to a sanitarium for drug addicts and I looked up his weight there. It's exactly ninety pounds."

Wentworth pushed himself to his feet. His side ached from a flesh wound and his right arm hung useless at his side, but there was a smile on his face. He put his good arm about Nita's shoulders.

"Darling," he said, "I think that—when I get out of the hospital—I shall go on a real bat!'

Nita shuddered, laughed up at him. "I'm willing, but for heaven's sakes, let's call it something... something else than... a bat!"

THE SPIDER

❏ #1: The Spider Strikes	$13.95
❏ #2: The Wheel of Death	$13.95
❏ #3: Wings of the Black Death	$13.95
❏ #4: City of Flaming Shadows	$13.95
❏ #5: Empire of Doom!	$13.95
❏ #6: Citadel of Hell	$13.95
❏ #7: The Serpent of Destruction	$13.95
❏ #8: The Mad Horde	$13.95
❏ #9: Satan's Death Blast	$13.95
❏ #10: The Corpse Cargo	$13.95
❏ #11: Prince of the Red Looters	$13.95
❏ #12: Reign of the Silver Terror	$13.95
❏ #13: Builders of the Dark Empire	$13.95
❏ #14: Death's Crimson Juggernaut	$13.95
❏ #15: The Red Death Rain	$13.95
❏ #16: The City Destroyer	$13.95
❏ #17: The Pain Emperor	$13.95
❏ #18: The Flame Master	$13.95
❏ #19: Slaves of the Crime Master	$13.95
❏ #20: Reign of the Death Fiddler	$13.95
❏ #21: Hordes of the Red Butcher	$13.95
❏ #22: Dragon Lord of the Underworld	$13.95
❏ #23: Master of the Death-Madness	$13.95
❏ #24: King of the Red Killers	$13.95
❏ #25: Overlord of the Damned	$13.95
❏ #26: Death Reign of the Vampire King	$13.95

THE MYSTERIOUS WU FANG

❏ #1: The Case of the Six Coffins	$12.95
❏ #2: The Case of the Scarlet Feather	$12.95
❏ #3: The Case of the Yellow Mask	$12.95
❏ #4: The Case of the Suicide Tomb	$12.95
❏ #5: The Case of the Green Death	$12.95
❏ #6: The Case of the Black Lotus	$12.95
❏ #7: The Case of the Hidden Scourge	$12.95

G-8 AND HIS BATTLE ACES

❏ #1: The Bat Staffel	$13.95

CAPTAIN SATAN

❏ #1: The Mask of the Damned	$13.95
❏ #2: Parole for the Dead	$13.95
❏ #3: The Dead Man Express	$13.95
❏ #4: A Ghost Rides the Dawn	$13.95
❏ #5: The Ambassador From Hell	$13.95

CAPTAIN ZERO

❏ #1: City of Deadly Sleep	$13.95
❏ #2: The Mark of Zero!	$13.95
❏ #3: The Golden Murder Syndicate	$13.95

OPERATOR 5

❏ #1: The Masked Invasion	$13.95
❏ #2: The Invisible Empire	$13.95
❏ #3: The Yellow Scourge	$13.95
❏ #4: The Melting Death	$13.95
❏ #5: Cavern of the Damned	$13.95
❏ #6: Master of Broken Men	$13.95
❏ #7: Invasion of the Dark Legions	$13.95
❏ #8: The Green Death Mists	$13.95
❏ #9: Legions of Starvation	$13.95
❏ #10: The Red Invader	$13.95
❏ #11: The League of War-Monsters	$13.95
❏ #12: The Army of the Dead	$13.95
❏ #13: March of the Flame Marauders	$13.95
❏ *NEW:* #14: Blood Reign of the Dictator	$13.95

DUSTY AYRES AND HIS BATTLE BIRDS

❏ #1: Black Lightning!	$13.95
❏ #2: Crimson Doom	$13.95
❏ #3: The Purple Tornado	$13.95
❏ #4: The Screaming Eye	$13.95
❏ #5: The Green Thunderbolt	$13.95
❏ #6: The Red Destroyer	$13.95
❏ #7: The White Death	$13.95
❏ #8: The Black Avenger	$13.95
❏ #9: The Silver Typhoon	$13.95
❏ #10: The Troposphere F-S	$13.95
❏ #11: The Blue Cyclone	$13.95
❏ #12: The Tesla Raiders	$13.95

DR. YEN SIN

❏ #1: Mystery of the Dragon's Shadow	$12.95
❏ #2: Mystery of the Golden Skull	$12.95
❏ #3: Mystery of the Singing Mummies	$12.95

MAVERICKS

❏ #1: Five Against the Law	$12.95
❏ #2: Mesquite Manhunters	$12.95
❏ #3: Bait for the Lobo Pack	$12.95
❏ #4: Doc Grimson's Outlaw Posse	$12.95
❏ #5: Charlie Parr's Gunsmoke Cure	$12.95